Saint Ettie's Music School

Saint Ettie's Music School

Martin Varny

British Library Cataloguing in Publication Data
A Record of this Publication is available from the British
Library

ISBN 978-1-914199-58-5

This edition published 2024 by The Red Telephone
Manchester, England

Music,

May it complete your happiness in the good times,
Lift your spirits in the dark times,
And always be there for you through the journey of life.

Dedicated to the orphans of this world, and those
who truly care for them.

Contents

Chapter 1

The door closed gently, like a dying kiss. The fingertips of her left hand did not move but remained touching the worn brass door handle, delaying the devastating moment for as long as possible when this tangible link with her dreams would be broken. With her right hand, she turned the heavy key one last time. She heard the lock click, withdrew the key, and turned to the man beside her. Still touching the brass door handle, she handed him the key.

"That's it then," the man said. "Everything is in the van now except for a few old instruments that we have left in one of the small storage rooms on the top floor. All the furniture and the good instruments are going to the new music school on the other side of the city."

His words were painful, and her throat tightened. She loved her instruments. They had been her life. The beautiful music she had heard them create, the children that they had inspired. They had been her source of fulfilment, her dreams and her happiness.

"Have to get going now," the man continued. He walked down the steps, got into the large van, which then drove away. She closed her eyes for a second, knowing the awful moment had come. Taking a sharp breath, she took her fingertips off the door handle, quickly turned, and went down the steps. At the last step, she hesitated, willing herself to go on, but she couldn't. She had promised herself that she wouldn't do this, but she couldn't help it. Turning around, she swept her eyes over the decaying façade of the building. The brick grimy from decades of fumes, the windows spotted with dusty rain, the paintwork on the window frames faded and, in some places, peeling off, and then her eyes switched and settled on the board. The green and gold sign had seen better days, but there was still something inspiring, dignified and majestic about it. The flowing letters revealed the now empty building's name in elderly splendour:

Saint Etheldreda's Music School
Established 1923

The final, irreversible step to the pavement broke the bond with all she had loved and dreamed of. Had she not suffered enough? Were the agonies of her childhood going to follow her forever? The words of self-pity filled her mind. The strongbox holding all the painful memories of her childhood, the place where she had put them away in order to forget, sprang open.

The loneliness of an only child, always nervous, often feeling she was not worth anything, and that it would be better if she was not there at all. The terrible discovery, overheard during one of her parents' bitter arguments, that they had never wanted children, her difficulty in making friends, the dark place her mind lived in most of the time, which could change in minutes by wild mood swings, all went round and round in an endless loop, battering her like hammers breaking stones. The escape from this unhappy, loveless place were her weekly piano lessons. There she was in another world. Confident, she lost herself in the melodies her slim fingers made when gliding over the ivory-coloured keys. Only later, on her own at college studying the music she loved, only there had she felt more settled. She was still damaged. The sudden changes in her mind that could take her from a happy place to a black cellar of danger had never gone away. Maybe that would never change, but the time spent in the dark places was less than it had been before. There at the college, the birds of hope had started to fly, and she had been able to open the door to her little world of dreams.

Now all that was gone, smashed into a million pieces

and thrown to the four winds. Head bowed and shoulders hunched, she began walking down the street to the bus stop. It was a dismal day. The sky, low with unbroken dark grey clouds, added to the burden of sadness she was already struggling to carry. Fallen autumn leaves, brown and curled, swirled and rustled over the road and pavement in the cold breeze. Others gathered in small, forlorn heaps in nooks and crannies, their lives over, their work done. All that remained for them was the final farewell, crushed to powder underfoot or ground into a muddy pulp in the gutters by passing wheels. The sad, mournful scene was a portrait of her inner self.

The bus finally arrived, and as it carried her back to her home, her eyes looked through the widows, but they did not see anything. Like a robot, with no memory of getting off the bus or walking the short distance to her apartment, she found herself standing in front of her door with the key in her hand. She opened the door, took off her coat and let it fall to the floor. It covered the mail lying on the mat, but she did not notice or care. Kicking off her shoes, she left them where they fell. She went into her bedroom and sat on the corner of her bed. For a few moments she did not move but stared down at her hands, looking at her fingers, wondering when they would ever touch the keys of a piano again. Her treasured old, upright piano, whom she had named Peggy, was gone. During the countless hours they had spent alone together, she would talk to Peggy as her dearest and closest friend, telling her about her joys, her sorrows, her dreams, her plans and her problems. Peggy knew more about her than anyone else in the whole world.

But now Peggy was in another place, and she was alone. The robotic spell broke. In an uncontrollable spasm, she took a short sharp intake of breath. Her throat tightened; her eyes hot. The lake of tears she had held in the dark clouds behind her eyes, now so heavy they could be held no more. Large, warm, heavy droplets, tinged with salt, gushed from her eyes and ran down her pale face. Half turning, she fell face down onto her white cotton pillow. Her lungs emptied in half choked gasps and refilled with strangled rasps through her constricted throat. Her shoulders heaved and her body shuddered with each agonising cycle. In total distress, Miss Elizabeth Rose wished the world would stop spinning.

But Elizabeth did not know. She didn't know that Peggy had heard and understood every word she had ever said to her. Elizabeth had never heard the story of Peggy's life, nor the suggestions she had sometimes made, or the words of comfort she had uttered when Elizabeth was feeling low. She had never heard Peggy's joy at the sounds she made from her keys and strings because Elizabeth could not hear her. But Peggy didn't mind. This was the way it was. There was a very old myth that some people could hear the instruments talk and could understand what they were saying, but Peggy only ever knew of one instrument that believed in it. But Peggy had an instinct, an inkling deep within her that said maybe, just maybe, if all the little pieces of a picture, especially if the piece that was the myth was really true, if all those pieces, now separately floating and drifting around the galaxy of destiny all came together at the right time and in the right place, then she and Elizabeth would meet again.

11

Chapter 2

The violin had been around for a long, long time. Her colour had faded and she had plenty of nicks and scratches, but she could still produce sounds that could touch even the hardest of hearts. She had been played by gifted musicians in many great concert halls and had risen to the top to be a first chair violin. She had developed a tough skin and, when necessary, a sharp tongue as she had to lead the orchestra and keep the other instruments in line. Her name was Veronica, and she believed the myth that people could hear them talk was true.

Over time, the hands she passed through became less gifted, less careful, less interested, until one day, soft hands had tenderly lifted her from the shelf in the second-hand music shop and taken her to Saint Etheldreda's Music School. The hands that held her now were young, some gentle, some rough, but she was happy that she still had the chance to inspire. So long as she still had that, she was content.

Now, leaning awkwardly against the cold wall of the grim storeroom, Veronica was afraid. The bare wooden floorboards, bare whitewashed walls and the small, dirt-streaked window that had last seen a cleaner more than twenty years ago, completed the terrifying feeling of being abandoned. The heavy footsteps coming in and out of the room together with the loud thuds, clangs and bumps, increased her anxiety with every passing minute. There were other instruments around her, but in the dim light it was very difficult for her to see who they were. She realised from her own strings, two broken only hours ago by uncaring hands, they must be the instruments nobody wanted, the ones left behind to slowly decay after years of faithful service.

The footsteps moved away and silence descended with the last muffled bang of the door at the end of the corridor. For some minutes all was quiet, no sound, no movement, just stillness.

Then, nervously, Veronica whispered, "Who's here?"

After a moments silence came a reply.

"Hi Veronica," said a deep voice. "It's me, Danny double bass. Nice to know you are still here to boss us around. That's the first time I have ever heard you sound scared."

"Oh Danny," said Veronica breathing a huge sigh of relief. "It's great to know you're here. I know I am supposed to be the strong one being the first violin, but I can't help feeling scared. I am so happy to hear your voice."

"Well thanks, Veronica. That must be the nicest thing you ever said to me." In a soft, very humble and sincere voice he added, "Real glad you're here with me, Veronica. This is a real bleak place. You in here too Daphne double bass?" he called anxiously. The silence gave the answer.

One by one, the instruments made themselves known. There were four more violins, Vera, Violet, Verity and Vivianne together with Celia cello, Teddy trombone, Charles clarinet, Theodore trumpet and the Bowie family.

"Bowies," cried Veronica in genuine delight. "Are you still all together?"

"Yes Ma'am, there's me, Blake, Belle my other half, and the kids Bibi, Bianca, Bettie, Beryl and Bridget. They kept us bows together 'cause we're a bit old-style; we do things the old-fashioned way. Who said old values don't pay off? It sure kept us together as a family. Then, sighing, he continued in a sad voice, "Well, if this is the end of the line, then at least we can talk with old friends to make the passing easier." His words were sharp in the minds of the other instruments, bringing a chill to their spirits.

"Is that everyone? Is there anyone else here?" asked Veronica.

For a moment it was still and then came a single word, "Us."

"Who?" said Veronica, startled by the unexpected reply.

"Us," said the voice again. "You don't know us honey, cause we ain't part of your set-up. We're from another department, another age, another sound. We go with the beat, got no conductor, do our own thing. No rules, babe, just the sound, the lights, the beat. You know what I'm sayin'? You follow the groove?"

"Who are you?" cried Veronica, amazed by a style she'd never heard before and not understanding much of what she was hearing.

"You do music?"

"Like you never heard before," said a beautiful luminous body. "I'm Garry, and together with my great pals Gilbert, Dean and his Caley family kit, we're a band, a group. We play rock an' roll."

"What on earth is rock an' roll?" asked Veronica.

"Well babe, you guys an' gals play all the old-fashioned sounds to well-dressed folk at fancy concert places. We play modern music, any place, anytime, we don't care. We play to young kids in jeans and leather jackets. So long as we got juice, we can get it all together."

"What sort of juice you talkin' about mister?" asked Verity, in her best southern belle manner. "You talkin' fruit or what?"

"Looks fruity enough to me, what I can see of him," said Violet. "I mean, look at his colour. Seems he's been washing in it."

"Back off ladies," said Garry sharply. "No need to make fun of us 'cause we're different to you. By juice folks, we mean electricity."

"Oh," said Verity. "Now we all know what your talkin' about. Never heard it called juice before."

14

"Me and my pal Gilbert here, we're electric guitars," continued Garry. I'm a lead guitar and Gilbert is a bass. We need juice to work properly. We need it for the amps."

"Amps?" queried Vivianne. "They some sort of monkeys?"

"Nope," said Garry. "Amp is short for amplifier. It's a piece of kit that makes the sounds louder. If you play outside to a thousand people, you got to have a few big powerful amps or hardly anyone gonna hear ya. You get the drift? It's big sound, honey, got to get the people moving, get the rhythm, get the beat. You need power."

"Not exactly cultural is it then," drawled Charles. "Just a lot of loud noise."

"Each to his own, man," murmured Gilbert. "Live and let play."

"So, Dean," said Veronica. "Is that you in the corner looking like a rolled over wedding cake holding up some sort of shiny umbrella? Can't see you too clearly, but to me, you look a very strange sort of instrument."

"If you want to talk to me, stringy babe," shot back Dean, "then don't talk down to me like you some sort of royalty. Your kind may have been around a while, but I don't take any of the hoity toity rubbish from the likes of you. People bin banging drums for a long time too, so forget the imperial attitude."

"Guys and gals," shouted Theodore. "Calm down. Here we are, stuck in this place for glory only knows how long, maybe forever, so let's try to get along and have a bit of respect for each other."

"I'm sorry, Dean," said Veronica. "I did not mean to be rude."

"That's OK," replied Dean. "After all, how are you supposed to know if you never seen our kind before? Let me tell you about me then. As you now know, my name is Dean, and I am the drum section of the band. This big beautiful baby in the middle is the bass, this one here is a snare drum and these two fellers are tom-toms. Up here we got the Caley family, lovely, brassy cymbals. Our job is to give the beat, the rhythm. Dependin' on the effect, I got different sticks and brushes to use, so this little old drum kit lady is real versatile."

"I stand humbled and corrected," replied Veronica. "I suppose being leader of the orchestra has made me a bit big-headed over the years."

"Ex-leader," Violet reminded her. "It's been some while since you played in a concert. You bin here at this school nearly as long as I have. Sorry, ex, closed down school. But yeah, OK Veronica, you know your stuff and have always looked after the rest of us, but the situation is a bit different now."

"You can bet your strings on that," drawled Verity. "Haven't known such quiet since I went for a facelift in some workshop, and boy, that was a while ago."

"None of us is getting' any younger darlin'," sighed Vera. "Hope this ain't gonna be the last finale, the last encore, the last." She stopped, desperate to retain control of herself. She willed herself not to cry.

"What kind of music do you play, Garry?" asked Charles. "Not Mozart or Bach, I suppose."

"Mozibark? Way out man. Sort of canine. Teeth. Yeah, could be a whole new sound," said Gilbert, from another planet. "Need to give that some thought."

Charles looked at him, very confused.

"Don't judge him too fast," said Garry. "He didn't get much schooling with his folks always on the road an' all. Yeah, I heard of Mozart, but classical stuff ain't our thing, man. It's the 1960s not the 1860s. We're into rock and roll. You heard of Bill Haley, The Drifters, Elvis? That's our scene, man. Rock and roll."

"Wow," said Violet. "I would love to hear your sound sometime."

"Not much chance of that happening the way things seem to be right now," Dean replied.

A silence then descended as if each of them knew that maybe no hands would ever touch them again. Their days of creating music were over. The stillness was accompanied by the increasing gloom, as darkness overtook the room and subdued it.

Chapter 3

They had reacted in fury. Angry and defiant, some shouting, others with cool force and two in tearful confusion, they had protested their innocence They denied the claim they had started the fire as a prank that had got out of control, but the men asking the questions did not seem to believe them. The owners of the building were demanding a lot of money from the city Juvenile Support Department to repair the damage.

He scanned all the children's faces. They had surrendered their fighting spirit and now, as unmoving as statues, their faces gave the message that they no longer cared.

"You are not here to be punished. Neither are you here because nobody believes you. I requested your presence here because I do not want you to think you are unimportant or left out. I want you to hear it from my lips that I, and the ladies and gentlemen sitting in front of you, have one simple purpose: we are here to help you. We will not talk about the fire today. That will not be talked about until the investigation as to how it started has been concluded."

The dark pink lips that showed no hint of meanness, closed. They were part of a face, lined by many summers, topped by receding, swept-back silver hair, a short, straight nose and grey piercing eyes that missed nothing. The face belonged to the Hawk. Shrouded in the black gown of his office, he was a judge at the Juvenile Justice Court. He had gained his nickname of the "Hawk" when he was a lawyer, due to his ability to swoop down very quickly on anybody he thought was lying. For anyone caught in the talons of his never-ending questions, there was no escape. Now, well past retirement age, he no longer heard criminal or lengthy civil cases, but had agreed to continue working as a judge in the Juvenile Justice Court on a part-time basis.

18

The Juvenile Justice system was there to provide rehabilitation and protective supervision for young people under eighteen years of age. The court hearings were informal, without the drama and theatre of criminal and other courts, and the judges could use their own experience on how each case was handled.

The Hawk resumed talking.

"Mr Robson," he said, addressing a gentleman sitting at the table in front of the children.

"Yes, your honour," said the man, rising to his feet.

"I understand you are the officer from the Juvenile Support Department involved with this case."

"That is correct, your honour," Mr Robson replied.

"Although I have tried to speak in simple terms," continued the Hawk, "I would ask you to talk now with the children to make sure each and every one of them has understood what I have just said. Please take your time." He then looked down at the two piles of papers on his desk, one with details about the boys and the other about the girls. The information included pictures of the children and their names, together with notes he had made from their files.

All the children had the same surname of "Brock" which was the name of the person who started the group of care homes at which the children lived. His name had been James Brock. It was the new policy of these care homes to give them all the same surname in order to make them feel part of a family. They were told their real names, if they were known, when they reached eighteen years of age and could leave. The idea was that hopefully, by then, they would be mature enough not to create any problems with any distant relatives they may find.

Starting with the boys, the Hawk looked at each of their faces and studied his notes.

Brandon:

16 years of age. Found abandoned as a baby. Mature for his age. Responsible, steady and reliable. Could be obstinate and impatient.

Max:

14 years of age. Single Parent: Mother, dead from drug overdose. Taken into care aged 1 year. Energetic. Outgoing. Could be silly. Liked playing pranks.

Jake:

13 years of age. Found abandoned as baby. Studious. Intelligent. Could be pessimistic and moody.

Harvey:

13 years of age. Parents, died in house fire (drug addicts). Taken into care after surviving house fire aged 1year. Back injured and scarred by burns. Shy. Secretive. Persistent. Could get very angry when annoyed. Unable to do sporting activities.

Alexander:

12 years of age. Found abandoned as a baby. Lively. Boisterous. Rowdy. Could be rude and abrasive.

Zac:

11 years of age. Given up for adoption as a baby. Parents: single mother (very young). Not adopted. Placed in permanent care home aged 7 years. Cheerful disposition. Mischievous. Could be disrespectful and quarrelsome.

The Hawk put down the pages and picked up the information about the girls. He looked at the youngest and thought she appeared about six years old instead of the nine years she was.

Rachael:

13 years of age. Taken into care aged 2 years. Parents, drug

addicts. Cheerful disposition. Affectionate. Caring. Could be stubborn and difficult.

Evie:

12 years of age. Given up for adoption as a baby. Single parent– mother. Not adopted. Placed in permanent care home aged 7 years. Quiet. Patient. Could be fussy.

Freya:

11 years of age. Taken into care aged 2 years. Parents both in prison (armed robbery & murder). Quiet, studious, above average intelligence. Easily irritated and angered by silliness.

Faith:

11 years of age. Parents drug addicts. Taken into care aged 1year. Artistic. Patient. Shy. Could be sulky.

Grace:

10 years of age. Found abandoned as a baby. Fun loving. Fearless. Mischievous. Could be cheeky and quarrelsome.

Jasmine:

10 years of age. Found abandoned as a baby. Cheerful disposition. Lively. Mischievous. Could be stubborn and hot-headed.

Emily:

9 years of age. Parents died in car accident. Child survived accident. Taken into care aged 6 years. Mentally fragile, can have periods of depression, anxiety and sleep problems (nightmares). Can be angry and sullen.

By the time the Hawk had refreshed his memory, Mr Robson had returned to his seat.

"Now for the most pressing priority," the Hawk began. Addressing Mr Robson, he asked what actions were taking place to provide a new home for the children.

"At present, your honour, we only have something temporary at another care home. We are looking hard and quickly to find something permanent and so far, we have found two possible locations. The first contact has been made with the present owners. Both owners prefer to rent their properties to us, but we would prefer to buy. This is due to alterations that may have to be carried out to make the property fit for its intended use. Owning the property makes this much easier."

"Very well," said the Hawk. "Please keep the court informed and I will instruct my clerk to contact you for another meeting in four weeks' time. For the moment then, unless there is anything else you wish to bring to my attention, this hearing is adjourned."

The Juvenile Support Officer and the two colleagues with him said they had no further points to raise at this time.

The Hawk stood up, collected his papers, wrapped his gown around him and left the room.

The winter was slowly fading and signs of spring were beginning to appear. Mr Robson and his two assistants had returned to the Juvenile court. This time the Hawk held the meeting in his chambers. After greeting them, the Hawk began the hearing, the court stenographer making a record of everything that was said.

"Thank you for your reports to the court concerning the new home for the children involved in this case," he began. "Firstly, what is happening at the moment with the children? Are they still attending school? How are they reacting to their temporary home?"

"The temporary home we are using, which is by no means ideal, is close enough to the previous place where they lived so they have been able to continue going to the same schools," Mr Robson answered. "With regard to their reactions, the situation could be better. The other children in the home are very young, less than five years old, so the staff are finding it rather stressful coping with much older children. They also seem to be impatient, bored and frustrated. Their behaviour has, at times, been disruptive. We have kept them informed of our progress, but this does not seem to have helped very much."

"That is worrying," said the Hawk. "As far as I understand the present situation," he continued, "a building has been found to make a new home, but changes are necessary to some of the rooms to make it suitable and fit for the intended purpose. How is this work going, and when do you expect everything to be finished?"

"Well, your honour," said Mr Robson. "We managed to find a property quite quickly and, after a lot of talking, we managed to persuade the owner to sell the building to us. This has made it possible for us to carry out the necessary changes to the building, which we hope will be completed within the next two weeks."

"Have staff been employed to live and work at the new home?" enquired the Hawk further.

"We are busy with new staff as we speak, your honour" replied Mr Robson. "We are hoping to make all appointments by the end of this week."

"Good," replied the Hawk. "Please keep the court informed when you are ready to move the children to the new home. We will meet again around that time. As to the matter of the fire, I still have not yet received the investigation report from the fire department. I will inform you when progress has been made with that matter. So, if there is nothing further, I will keep you no longer."

After leaving the court and returning to his office, Mr Robson received an urgent telephone call. His faced tensed and took on an angry expression. He put on his coat and some twenty-five minutes later he was standing in front of the children.

"Your behaviour is not acceptable," he shouted in fury. "The principal of this home where we have temporarily put you has had enough. You leave me no choice. I am going to split you up and send you to different places as soon as I can arrange it. We will find another use for the new home we were busy preparing for you as it seems you are unable to control yourselves enough to remain together."

Thirteen mouths dropped open in shock, and twenty-six wide-open, staring eyes were filled with fear.

Chapter 4

Dust, as yet not thick, covered the instruments with a grey skin of neglect.

"Oh my," sighed Verity. "This everlasting quiet is getting to me. I never thought I'd say it but I miss the noise, the kids who used to come here, even the rough-and-ready brutes like that kid with fingers like bananas and who smelt like a drain."

"Even that beefy guy with the red hair?" asked Vivianne. "He'd grab you round the throat like trying to strangle you, and then tried to saw you in half."

"You're telling us?" chorused the Bowie girls. "Every time he broke one of your strings, which happened so often, we got whipped." They continued reminiscing, as that was all they could do to keep cheerful.

"Shush everyone." Veronica cried out. "Did you hear that noise?"

In the silent room, every ear was highly tuned. The silence remained.

"I could have sworn I heard something," Veronica said.

Every instrument stayed silent, listening with intense concentration, but no sound came.

"Must be dreaming," said Veronica, even though she was sure she had heard something. "Carry on with your story, Teddy"

"It's funny," said Teddy. "Some of the performances I remember best were when some disaster happened, yet the audiences seemed to love it. I remember one time when we were playing a really fast piece. All the elbows of the players were going like pistons on a steam engine, and my player was yanking my slide up and down like he was pumping for oil. Anyway, a violinist in front of me was really swaying to the rhythm and his chair kept tilting back and forth. My player was moving around a lot as well and then it happened.

25

My slide got hooked behind the violinist's chair leg, and when my player pulled back my slide, the chair tipped over and a whole section of the orchestra went over like dominoes. I don't know how, but we never missed a beat. A cello player got his bow stuck in a violinist's ear so that his head shot from side to side like a ping-pong ball. At the same time, a bassoon player was getting his cheeks bashed in by two violin bows. The conductor really got into the spirit by dropping to his knees every few seconds to keep the players on the floor in time with the rest of the orchestra. The audience loved it, as they thought it was part of the performance. At the end, the bassoon guy looked like he had just gone fifteen rounds in a boxing fight; the violinist couldn't stop moving his head from side to side for a week and one lady actually changed professions and became a contortionist. The only sad thing was what happened to Theresa. Anybody know Theresa Triangle?"

"Heard of her," said Violet. "Didn't she have to retire quite early?"

"Yeah," replied Teddy. "That was because of what happened to her that night. The young lady who was playing her was very slight; had long hair, and used to wear high stiletto heel shoes to make herself look a bit taller. When the domino effect happened, she got catapulted across the stage and one of her stilettos went straight through one of the footlights. Well, there was a great blue flash; her long hair went straight up about four feet and started to weave and twist around like a load of dancing snakes. Sparks started flying off poor Theresa like a truckload of sparklers catching fire. The player's hand was shaking around so fast that Theresa was going off like an electric bell. It wasn't until a fuse blew that she could stop. Real pity as she was a really nice lady, but she never got over it. She started getting nervous twitches, was constantly charged up, and she stayed hot for months. She stopped getting invited out as her behaviour got really shocking. A big shame, really."

"Great story Teddy," said Verity. "Something similar happened to me early on in my career. We were performing *The Ocean Suite* by Victor Vol-au-Vent in a really old concert hall, which turned out to be an appropriate piece for what happened later. The concert hall looked smart and well cared for, but actually it was more or less falling down. As you know, there is a big piano part and they had managed to get The Grand Duchess Petula. You ever met her? Charming lady. Great gleaming black beauty she was, and when her lid was up, she was every inch an aristocrat. Not that she was at all stuck up. She was a real lady, and was always happy to talk and help whoever you were, especially the new, inexperienced instruments. The guy playing her that night was that famous Italian, Alberto Pastaslurpi.

"Anyway, we were reaching the finale of the piece and Alberto was really going some. Petula was a shakin' and vibratin' and giving it her all, when suddenly there was a groan, a crack, and then a great bang. Half of Petula's big front leg went through the floor right up to her knee. She stayed there at an angle for a couple of minutes but Alberto somehow kept going. Mind you, the conductor was Sir George Gnasherbrush and nothing, but nothing, seemed to faze him. Real old school, army, stiff upper lip, the genuine article. We used to call him "GeeGee" as a nickname, but there was no horsing around with him, if you'll forgive the pun. Like I said, it stayed like that for a couple of minutes and then there was another crash, and the whole of Petula's leg disappeared. It seems that when she first went down, her leg rested on a water pipe under the stage. Think it was from the fire sprinkler system. Anyway, this had broken under Petula's weight and suddenly a great jet of water burst through the floor right underneath the chair of the first violinist. Up he went, about ten feet. Both his chair and he himself were suspended on this water jet. Old GeeGee, well, he never even blinked. He kept going and even made sure the first violinist could see his baton so that everyone kept together. There was water all over the place, and the whole stage looked like a load of paddling pools with a "giant fountain in the middle.

The next thing was that the two trumpets, standing on the far side of the orchestra, came into action. As they started, two jets of water came out of them like water cannons on a fire engine and headed straight for GeeGee. Despite his age, old GeeGee sure could move quick. He ducked, and the two water jets converged and belted into one of the side stage spotlights. First there was a fizz, followed by a great bang, and an arc of vivid blue light that cracked its way at the speed of light to the ceiling above the stage. That started off a gigantic pyrotechnic display with blue flashes and bangs and poppin' noises. I tell ya, it was mighty awesome. And you know what? Alberto never stopped playing, we never stopped playing. GeeGee did not seem to notice any of it even though three violins and a cello had floated off down the stage steps and were playing from the front row of the audience. The drum player, who couldn't swim and was as white as a sheet, was sitting on his drum, which was spinning round and round, and Petula kept giving it the works, even though she looked like a ship going down.

"Eventually, someone managed to turn off the water valve. The first violinist came down with a crash, still playing mind you, and the trombone managed to stay with us by hooking himself round the neck of a double bass as the water surged away through the floor like a tremendous drain. Somehow or other we finished the piece, and just as GeeGee brought down his baton for us to stop, the last of the stage lights blew up with a great bang like a battleship firing all its guns at once.

"The stage was pitch black. Some of the guys started to get up and make for the stage door but GeeGee told them to sit down as he hadn't finished yet. For about thirty seconds, there was dead silence. You could hear a pin drop. We wondered if the audience had already gone home. Then a spotlight on the balcony burst into life and lit up the stage. It looked like a bomb site. Old GeeGee slowly turned to face the audience. He carefully smoothed back his hair, and then made a deep bow.

"At that moment, the audience erupted. They went wild. They were jumping up and down, clapping, and shouting encore. They seemed to think it was part of the performance. GeeGee turned and, with a sweeping open arm, presented us, the orchestra, to the audience. As the crowd clapped even harder, GeeGee applauded us too. Glory knows what we looked like, but it did not seem to matter to anyone. Even the critics were fooled as it was the best review I ever read. Apparently, the locals gave the place a nickname afterwards and called it Hurricane Hall."

"That sure must have been some night, Verity," laughed Vivianne. "I've always been a bit scared of all that electric stuff though. I heard a few horror stories about exploding lights."

"Yeah," chipped in Gilbert. "When you got electric problems, it sure can be spectacular. We had it once with an amp. Something must have got busted, probably after being thrown around on trucks all the time going between different places. Anyway, we were really cranking it up to its limits when up it went like a firework display. Awesome man, awesome, we blacked out an entire neighbourhood for six hours."

"Say you guys, Garry, Gilbert, Dean," asked Veronica. "How come you ended up at the music school anyway? The rest of us have all been around for a long, long time, but you guys are really young."

"Bit sad, really," replied Garry. "We started off with three young kids who were really into rock. They had money, as they all had rich daddies. Only problem was, the rich daddies didn't like rock and roll – didn't like the whole scene, man. Anyway, they found out that the kids were going off at weekends playing music all hours of the day and night. They also found out the kids had been experimentin' with strange substances and they really got mad. They wanted the kids to stay on the straight and narrow, go to college, become lawyers and stuff. So, the daddies chucked us on the back of a pickup truck and took us downtown, back to the music store, and tried to get their money back. They did not have much luck, so they dumped us at the city garbage depot. Luckily, someone saw them 'cause the next thing we know we're here."

"That's a real shame," said Violet. "A real crying."

"Shush, quiet," interrupted Veronica sharply. "Did you hear that?"

"What?" said Charles.

"Not sure," replied Veronica, "but it sounded like footsteps."

They all listened intently.

"There," whispered Veronica. "There it is again."

"Yeah," whispered Danny, "I heard that too."

"Stay quiet everybody, act like you're dead," commanded Veronica in a stern whisper.

"May as well be, rotting here," giggled Vera.

Veronica glared at Vera.

They heard a door open and then close in the distance. Then another, but this time closer and they could now hear the footsteps and the voices, all getting closer and closer and closer.

The door of the room creaked open.

Chapter 5

Miss Abigail Stratton sat at her desk, combing her fingers through her short grey hair while studying the last piece of paperwork in front of her. Her nose was straight and slim, and her reading glasses had the annoying habit of sliding down, causing her to lose focus. She pushed them back with a short, decisive movement of her middle finger and her clear, grey eyes continued reading. She had just returned from the Juvenile Court where she had been to a meeting with the judge hearing the case of the fire and the thirteen children that would very soon be placed in her care. Mr Robson, a colleague from the Juvenile Support Department, had also been present. Miss Stratton was a gifted organiser, which was why she had been asked to set up the new care home called Saint Etheldreda's Foundation.

Like a coin, her personality had two different sides, each with its own strengths and weaknesses. One side was strong, straightforward and decisive. Her total self-confidence was shown by a huge amount of stubborn determination and complete fearlessness when trying to complete her plans. At times she was unbendable, and she had a commanding presence which sent out a message that she was not to be played around with. Her battles against silly rules were well known. She had little time for pettiness but had no time for sloppiness in the written word and bad manners. For a short time, she had been to a small school where the headmistress, who tolerated many childish pranks, had, even though it was a school for girls, chosen the school's motto of, "Manners Maketh Man" and she made sure none of her pupils ever forgot it.

The other side was gentler. Her patience could last for days and she could accept other people's opinions even when she disagreed with them. She was a good listener, and she tried not to jump to conclusions without thinking. The largest and most complicated part on this side of the coin of her character was shaped by her past. In her early twenties, she had been lost in love with a young man and they had planned to marry and have a large family together. The tragedy of his death had sent Miss Stratton to a grim place and she had lost her way. Treasuring his memory, she had turned her back on romance and accepted that without him she did not want children of her own. Over time, she began to crave for an outlet to give her fulfilment. Step-by-step, the heat of her love for children burned through the dark walls that surrounded her, and it led her to dedicate her life to children who, for whatever reason, had never had the love of a family.

Returning all the paperwork to a cardboard file, Miss Stratton got up from her desk, walked out of her office and knocked on the next door down the corridor.

A cheerful voice said, "Come in" and Miss Stratton entered the bright office. Her young assistant, Miss Marigold, stood up to greet her.

"Hello, Miss Stratton," she said.

"Good afternoon, Miss Marigold," replied Miss Stratton, smiling. "Please sit down. I don't want you to keep jumping up every time I come in. This is not the army," she said with a big smile.

Miss Stratton had only known Miss Marigold for about two weeks, but even within that short space of time they had found a strong connection between them. Miss Marigold was in her early twenties, with dark brown hair cut in a modern bob style. It curved around her face and appeared stuck to her cheeks in order to keep its perfect shape. Her brown, intelligent eyes flashed with cheerfulness, and her long slim fingers could race around a typewriter faster than anyone Miss Stratton had ever seen. She was an optimist, always willing to learn new skills, very loyal, and she had a hatred of letting people down. A promise was a promise, and she worked for perfection in all the tasks she did. She had been abandoned as a baby and grown up in a care home, and this had taught her to see what was important and what were just ornaments of vanity. One day she hoped she would find romance, but until that happened, she found contentment in her work. It gave her the pleasure of somehow repaying her debt to those like Miss Stratton, who had given their lives to helping such as her to make the best of their abilities.

"What is the situation with the local schools Miss Marigold?" Miss Stratton began. "We need to get the children's education sorted out as quickly as we can."

"There are five schools in the area, Miss Stratton," said Miss Marigold, "and so far, I have managed to contact four of them. The secretary at one of the school's I contacted, said that their headmaster, a Mr Chalmers, is away at a conference, and he does not get back until the end of the week. I gave the secretary some details about the Foundation and the children, and she said they would be back in touch with us as soon as they could. I will contact the last school over the next few days. So far," continued Miss Marigold, "the responses we have had have not been very good. Two of the schools are already full to the point of overflowing and they just do not have the room for any more children. The other school made a lot of excuses as to 'fitting in problems' that may happen with our children."

"Such as?" asked Miss Stratton.

"Oh, maybe our children are troublemakers, or are different in other ways to the children they already have."

"I see," said Miss Stratton. She had met this type of prejudice many times in the past and was well battle-hardened in fighting against it. She had a long list of victories in this area, but it took time, energy and a lot of effort. "Very well," continued Miss Stratton. "Contact the remaining school, but don't waste too much time begging. We have other priorities. Let me know what happens, but let's plan for the situation where we will teach the three Rs ourselves. We will see what our children know and how they react. After that, we can do battle with the schools. Now, for the most important item, Miss Marigold. When are the children arriving?"

"Tomorrow at ten o'clock," replied Miss Marigold. "A bus has been arranged to bring them from their present care home to us."

"Thank you, Miss Marigold. It is not a moment too soon." She relayed the incident that had happened because of the children's behaviour at the temporary home and how Mr Robson had been on the edge of splitting them up, which had shocked them into being more sensible. "Well, I think that's all." Miss Stratton paused. "Oh, just one other thing, at the moment we are only using the first two floors of the building, the ground floor and the first floor. Have you inspected the upper floors?"

"Yes, Miss Stratton," replied Miss Marigold. "The second floor has seven rooms and two small bathrooms. The top floor, the third floor, has one large room, which takes up about two thirds of the area of the whole third floor. There is a door at the back of this large room which leads into a corridor where there are four small storage rooms. I have not been in the storage rooms to inspect them yet, but I will do so immediately if you wish."

"No, no," answered Miss Stratton. "They will keep for another time. Are all the doors upstairs locked?" she enquired.

"Indeed, they are Miss Stratton," replied Miss Marigold. "I've got all the keys here except the key for the cupboard in the hall where the cleaning ladies keep their mops, buckets, dusters and such like. There is only one key for the cupboard and the lady in charge of the cleaners has it," she concluded.

34

"Excellent," said Miss Stratton smiling. She got up, thanked Miss Marigold once again, and left the office to go and see Mrs Hutchins, the cook.

Miss Stratton had interviewed five people for the job as cook at Saint Etheldreda's Foundation and the choice had been easy. Mrs Hutchins had arrived wearing bright, confident clothes of red, white and green and her movements showed an energy of a much younger person. She had extensive experience of inventing and making meals in a large school kitchen but was still bursting with ideas. Describing the wholesome meals she could make, all packed with the goodness growing children needed, had Miss Stratton licking her lips in hunger. Her amusing comments, made with her blue eyes twinkling, showed her humour, and Miss Stratton had laughed out loud a few times. Now a widow, with her children and grandchildren no longer living in the area, Mrs Hutchins was searching for a position where she could live and work under the same roof. Miss Stratton had thought Mrs Hutchins was perfect for the job.

The kitchen was a good size: not too big, but spacious enough to have sufficient working space, plenty of cupboards, a big cooking stove, three good-sized sinks and room to fit a large table. The City authorities had really done an amazing job. A serving hatch had been fitted between the new kitchen and the original dining room next door.

"Good morning, Mrs Hutchins," greeted Miss Stratton warmly as she entered the kitchen.

"Oh, good morning, Miss Stratton," replied Mrs Hutchins.

"Everything to your satisfaction, Mrs Hutchins?"

"Oh yes," replied Mrs Hutchins. "It's perfect, couldn't wish for better."

"Wonderful," said Miss Stratton. "Now, the children will be arriving tomorrow at ten o'clock. Do you have any plans?"

"Yes," replied Mrs Hutchins. "I have made up these menus for you to take a look at and a list of groceries I can have delivered first thing tomorrow morning if you are happy with my suggestions."

Sitting down at the kitchen table, Mrs Hutchins showed Miss Stratton her menus which they immediately agreed on. Then they began to put together their ideas about rules for the children eating any snacks and the rota for the washing up that the children would be expected to do. When this had all been settled, Miss Stratton asked Mrs Hutchins if she had any ideas about something they could do to "break the ice" with the children on their first day. After a moment of thought, Mrs Hutchins came out with a suggestion. Miss Stratton's hand flew over her mouth, her eyes shot wide open, her eyebrows arched so high they nearly touched the top of her head, and she took a deep intake of breath.

"Oh, we couldn't possibly do that, Mrs Hutchins." gasped Miss Stratton, totally shocked. "That would give the wrong idea completely."

Mrs Hutchins looked calmly back at Miss Stratton. "Why not?" she said, her blue eyes twinkling. She began to outline how her idea would take place and asked what problem there could be with it. Taking her hand away from her mouth and concentrating hard, Miss Stratton thought about the idea that normally would have been totally alien to her. Then she lifted her head and looked at Mrs Hutchins. A smile began to form, which quickly changed into a wide grin and then finally a great peel of laughter broke from Miss Stratton's lips. "You know, Mrs Hutchins, that is an absolutely wonderful idea."

Chapter 6

Sadness and gloom had been replaced by wide-eyed curiosity and relief.

When the bus stopped, the thought of saying goodbye to friends made the children very sad. Then, as they were all told to leave the bus together, flickers of hope produced tentative smiles. Now they sat in a warm, brightly coloured room that had three sofas and seven straight-backed chairs. Although it was a big room, the amount of furniture inside made it cosy. Along one wall there were shelves filled with books, and in the middle of another wall was a table with a TV on it. All eyes were fixed on the tall, grey-haired lady, and the two other ladies who stood either side of her.

"My name is Miss Stratton," the tall lady began, "and the other two ladies standing with me are Miss Marigold, my assistant, and Mrs Hutchins, our cook. I would like to welcome you to your new home. We hope you will be happy here and that today will be a new start. I know the last few weeks have been difficult for you, but we will put all that behind us. It is our dream," she looked at Miss Marigold and Mrs Hutchins, "that together we can create in this building a family, a family where you are happy, safe and cared for so that when you leave here when you are eighteen, at least for this part, you can say to friends that you had a happy childhood. You may have seen on the board outside that this new home is called Saint Etheldreda's Foundation. Now," she continued, "we will show you upstairs to where you will sleep and the area where Miss Marigold, Mrs Hutchins and I live, so that you will know where to find us, and where the bathrooms are. Then we will show you where Miss Marigold's office, my office, the dining room, the room we will use as a temporary classroom and the kitchen are. We will explain the normal day-to-day living rules to you tomorrow. This does not mean that today you can start breaking the place up." She finished with a laugh.

Throughout this speech, the children had not moved, but now, they shot a few glances at each other before engaging in excited whispers.

"OK," said Miss Stratton. "Let's go upstairs so you can see your dormitories, choose your beds, and unpack your rucksacks. There are two dormitories, one for girls, the other for boys, and there are separate bathrooms with washbasins and showers. In the bathrooms you will also find cupboards on the wall where you can keep your toothbrushes," she concluded.

Mrs Hutchins went back to her kitchen, and Miss Stratton and Miss Marigold went upstairs with the children. They showed them where everything was, including the door to where they, the staff, lived. Miss Stratton, Mrs Hutchins and Miss Marigold all had their own separate bedrooms and bathrooms and they shared a comfortable sitting room. They also had a small kitchenette for making tea or coffee. After choosing their beds and getting themselves sorted out, Miss Stratton and Miss Marigold took the children back downstairs to the dining room. Opening the door, the children slowly filed in. Both ladies heard the little gasps of surprise. On the dining room table were bowls and plates containing a variety of cakes of all shapes and sizes, in every colour you could think of; some with cherries, some with nuts and others with chocolate sprinkles. There were buns and biscuits and jugs of lemonade. Mrs Hutchins had produced a feast.

Miss Stratton went to the head of the table, but the children held back a little, unsure of where to sit.

"Please come to the table and sit down, everyone," she said. "I expect you are all hungry, so our wonderful cook here has prepared something for you." She indicated with her arm the warm face of Mrs Hutchins who was peering through the kitchen hatch.

Jostling each other, they moved toward the chairs around the table, the oldest taking the chairs furthest away from Miss Stratton, who stood smiling at the scene. She knew what they were thinking. She was still an unknown quantity, so best to keep a bit of distance until they had figured her out.

When they were all seated, Miss Stratton said, "OK, help yourselves and enjoy these delicious cakes." To encourage them she leant over to a plate of doughnuts and took one. The children began whispering to each before helping themselves to the magnificent spread that Mrs Hutchins had created. The children started to talk to each other across the table and made little jokes, but they were still nervous and not very playful.

When the children had finished eating, Miss Stratton asked them to help her take the plates, glasses and cutlery into the kitchen.

Mrs Hutchins smiled on seeing the children carrying the crockery with such focus. "Just put them in the sink my loves, I'll sort it all out later."

Returning to the dining room, Miss Stratton asked them to take their seats again. Mrs Hutchins appeared and brought with her a large bowl of what looked like round cakes made of sponge in all sorts of colours. After three trips to the kitchen, a total of four bowls stood on the table. The children looked on with puzzled expressions on their faces. Miss Stratton stood up, slowly leant over the table and picked up a sponge ball. With a small smile on her face, she threw the cake at Grace and it landed on her head. Thirteen mouths dropped open. Thirteen pairs of eyes opened as wide as they would go.

"Come on Grace," said Miss Stratton with a wide smile. "I dare you."

Grace looked quickly at her friends around her and then, with lips pressed together in determination, she lunged over the table, grabbed a sponge ball and threw it back at Miss Stratton. The "bun fight" had begun.

Coloured sponge cakes flew across the room in all directions and everyone ran around taking cover wherever they could. It was Miss Stratton, Miss Marigold and Mrs Hutchins versus the children. Harvey, who due to his back problems, did not join in the throwing but instead scampered around on the floor and under the table, collecting fallen sponge balls to supply to the front-line troops with fresh ammunition. For half an hour the battle raged until exhausted and breathing hard, Miss Stratton pulled a white handkerchief from her pocket and started waving it above her head. "We surrender!" she shouted, "We surrender!"

A great cheer erupted from thirteen throats, arms started waving and hands punching the air. Chants of "We won, we won," echoed around the room. Miss Stratton, Miss Marigold and Mrs Hutchins sank to the floor. Panting, they laughed, patted each other on the arms and giggled like naughty children. The atmosphere in the room sparkled with gaiety. Babbling voices and shrieks of laughter created a room of relaxed happiness.

After a few minutes, Miss Stratton began to look at the battlefield. There were pieces of sponge cake everywhere. "OK everybody, did you enjoy the fun?" she shouted.

"That was great," shouted Grace, her friends nodding in agreement.

"Glad you enjoyed it," replied Miss Stratton. "Maybe now we should start cleaning the place up," she said.

Grace, still highly charged with adrenalin, shot back, "You lost, so you clean up." The room hushed and Miss Stratton, who was for a split second stunned by what Grace had just said, quickly recovered and, pretending to start crying, she wailed, "Oh Grace, are you going to be so cruel to us?"

Trying to copy Graces' daring, Jasmine cried out, "But you started it."

"Oh, please help us, please help us," Miss Stratton wailed. The children looked at each other and then Zac suddenly said, "We'll let Brandon decide. What do you think, Brandon?" All eyes turned to Brandon.

"Well," said Brandon with an expression of careful thought, stretching out the word for a second or two, "It could mean extra TV time."

"Or extra ice-cream," chipped in Rachael, who could never eat enough of it.

"Or extra sweets," added Faith.

"A trip to the movies," shouted Alexander.

Miss Stratton was giggling hard but after catching her breath replied, "I make no promises, but you kids sure do drive a hard bargain."

Brandon turned and muttered to Jake, who was sitting behind him, and then they both nodded.

"OK," he said. "We have big hearts, so we will give you a hand."

They began to collect all the sponge debris and put it into paper bags.

"What are you going to do with all this?" asked Freya, who had enjoyed the fight even though, at first, she thought it had been silly.

Miss Stratton had an answer for this, but instead of saying it she said, "I don't know Freya. Do you have any ideas?"

Freya thought for a moment and then said, "Maybe we could feed the birds?"

"Is there a park near here?" asked Harvey, who had heard what they were saying.

41

"Yes," replied Miss Stratton. "There is a park about ten minutes' walk from here.

"Are there ducks there as well?" asked Evie. "And maybe squirrels?"

"There is a big pond with ducks there, Evie," Miss Stratton replied, "but I am not sure about squirrels. We will go there on Saturday and at least give the birds and ducks a party." Miss Stratton was very pleased that the children had arrived at this idea on their own, as it is what she had planned all along.

One child now sat slightly apart from the rest of the children. Her face was sad, and she stared at some fixed point in front of her. Miss Marigold had glanced at her a few times after the bun-fight had finished and seen that the girl had become very quiet. Miss Marigold knelt by the young girl. She was not sure exactly how to handle the situation, but she knew the reason why this was happening. She had read the reports with all the information about each child that Miss Stratton had given her.

"Are you OK, Emily?" asked Miss Marigold in a very soft voice.

"Yes," answered Emily in a whisper.

Before Miss Marigold had a chance to say any more, Rachael appeared, sat down by Emily and put her arms around her.

"It's OK, Miss," murmured Rachael. "We can take care of Emily. We know she hurts a lot inside sometimes." Taking Emily's hand, Rachael led her back to the other girls.

Miss Marigold had to struggle not to cry. The motherly instinct that Rachael had just shown had touched her. Going back to Miss Stratton and Mrs Hutchins, Miss Marigold told them what had just happened.

"It's beautiful to see," said Mrs Hutchins. "They are close already. They really seem to care for each other."

The afternoon was nearly over. Going into the TV room,

Miss Stratton found the children watching a programme. "Are you hungry again yet?" she asked with a smile. They nodded, so Miss Stratton said, "OK then, come with me to the dining room." The children followed her and they sat down to a meal of tasty sandwiches followed by ice-cream. When they had finished eating, Mrs Hutchins asked them to help her clear away but said she would do all the washing up as it was their first day. Back in the TV room, the children were left to do what they wanted. Freya and Jake looked at all the books so see what was there. The rest of the children sat and watched TV. It had been a tiring day and by mid evening the children wanted to go to bed. Brandon went and found Miss Stratton and she went with the children up to their dormitories. She helped to get them settled and wished them good-night, saying they would get a call at eight o'clock the next morning. Leaving the girls' dormitory, Miss Stratton briefly glanced up. There, on the wall above the door, set in a beautiful frame, was a poster. The background of the poster was shades of green in a swirling pattern and the words were in gold, edged with red. Miss Stratton had seen the poster in a local shop and the words had made her remember. A long time ago, words like these had helped her so much through a dark time in her life.

She had bought two of the posters and had them framed using her own money. She had hung them above the doors in each dormitory with the thought that the children would see them every morning. Miss Stratton hoped that the words would either help them now, or that they would remember them and maybe help them at some point in their future lives. The words read:

> *TAKE COURAGE.*
> *YOU CAN MAKE IT.*

The routine life at Saint Etheldreda's Foundation began to settle down. Miss Stratton explained the few rules she had about punctuality, being tidy, the hours they could watch TV, doing school homework when that started to happen again, and the rotas for helping Mrs Hutchins in the kitchen. They went outside to become familiar with the area and went to the park to feed the birds and ducks with the leftover sponge cakes from the bun-fight. Emily had woken three times on different nights, her screaming panic triggered by the changes in her surroundings. Rachael had comforted her and settled her down as she had told Miss Stratton she would.

One afternoon, Miss Stratton was in her office when Emily knocked on the door.

"Miss," Emily began. "Can I ask you something?"

"Of course, Emily," Miss Stratton replied. "Please come in and sit down." Miss Stratton moved the chairs so they could sit side-by-side.

"What did you want to ask me, Emily?" said Miss Stratton.

"The picture in our bedroom; what do the words really mean?" Emily asked. Her wide eyes were full of curiosity.

"Well, Emily," replied Miss Stratton. "The words mean that if you are strong and brave, then you can be and do anything you want. If you are really sad, then if you are strong and brave, you can make yourself happy again."

The girl said nothing but looked thoughtful, her brain processing what she had heard and relating it to herself. She then came out with another question.

"Who was Saint Ettie Miss?" she asked.

"Not Saint Ettie, Emily, although I agree it is a lot easier to say," laughed Miss Stratton, "it's Saint Etheldreda."

"Yeah, yeah Saint Etheld... Oh, I can't say it; it's too complicated," said Emily.

"Never mind, Emily," said Miss Stratton with a warm smile, "it doesn't matter. Now," continued Miss Stratton, "that is a very good question, a very good question indeed young lady."

As soon as the words were out of her mouth, Miss Stratton realised that she had somehow touched something deep in Emily's mind. The child's face began to crumple and her lips began to quiver. Miss Stratton could see that Emily was fighting to control herself, but she was losing. The child brushed away a tear that had forced its way out and she sniffed hard. Miss Stratton moved quickly from her chair, went to Emily, put her arms around her and hugged her. Emily was shaking, and burying her head into Miss Stratton's shoulder; she burst into uncontrollable tears. The tears continued and the child gripped Miss Stratton's arm until her knuckles were white. The young girl's body was wracked with spasms and, although she did not make much noise, the power of her pain was obvious.

Miss Stratton swayed from side to side, holding Emily tight to her, but said nothing. She felt the girl trying to bring herself under control. Her wracking body slowed and became still. Eventually, the girl lifted her head and looked at Miss Stratton's face. The pain in her eyes was as plain as black on white. Her lips still quivered, but the movement began to stop. Miss Stratton released her hug, but she continued to hold Emily in her arms. She stroked the girl's hair and then with her clean, unused handkerchief, she wiped Emily's wet cheeks.

"You OK, Emily?" she whispered. The girl looked into Miss Stratton's eyes. She nodded and then sniffed.

"Blow your nose with this," said Miss Stratton, offering her handkerchief to the young girl.

Emily took it and blew her nose loudly. Rubbing the back of her hand across her eyes, down each cheek and under her nose, she slumped and relaxed.

"Did I say something that hurt you?" asked Miss Stratton

in a voice as gentle as a lamb. "What did I say Emily, that made you feel so sad?"

"You called me young lady," whispered Emily. "Only my mummy ever called me that, and I miss her, oh how I miss her." The tears began to run down her face again. Miss Stratton put her arms back around the girl and hugged her until the agonised sobbing stopped.

From the records in her possession, Miss Stratton knew of Emily's tragedy, of the sudden death of her young parents nearly three years ago in a car accident. The wounds were still raw, only just beneath the surface, and anything could trigger them.

"You OK, Emily?" asked Miss Stratton again, and Emily nodded.

"Shall I tell you about Saint Etheldreda now, or shall we wait and tell everybody in class tomorrow? Maybe it would be nice if everyone knew who she was as she is the patron of our Foundation."

Emily nodded again. "Yeah," she breathed, followed by a sniff, "tell us all tomorrow."

Miss Stratton smiled. "Do you want to go back to the others now?"

The girl hesitated and Miss Stratton sensed that Emily felt secure with her arms around her, a feeling of safety that maybe she had not felt for a long time. After a few minutes, Emily said she would like to go back with the others now, so Miss Stratton set her on her feet and Emily left the room. No sooner had she left the room, when Miss Stratton heard Emily whistling a short little tune as she walked back to the TV room. She had no idea at that moment where that short tune would lead them.

Chapter 7

The slim, sensitive fingers moved the piece of wire around the inside of the mechanism, and they translated what he felt into pictures in his mind. He found the part he knew must be there, took out the wire and replaced it with a shaped piece of stiff metal. He pushed the metal strip against the part the wire had found. It moved a fraction, so he pushed a bit harder. With a rush, the mechanism moved quickly, resulting in what, for Harvey, was a sharp metallic clunk of exhilaration. He turned the knob and, with a steady gentle push, opened the door. He peeked into the corridor behind the door and then he pulled it shut again. He did not want to go any further.

Harvey was only interested in his passion, and his passion was locks.

It had begun in a previous home where Harvey had become friends with a quiet boy who was about three years older than himself. Harvey had caught him opening the door to the kitchen store cupboard and, after agreeing not to tell anyone about it, the older boy began to teach Harvey about locks. Harvey was fascinated. His friend had an older brother who had also been in care, but now he was an apprentice in the maintenance department of a local factory. This older brother had, over time, given his younger brother some watch maker's files, two pairs of pliers and some odd strips of metal with which to make lock picks. He had given some of these tools to Harvey.

As if to make up for the injuries to his back, Harvey had incredibly sensitive fingers. He could feel around the inside of a lock with a piece of bent wire and he could see in his head what the wire was touching.

Kneeling now in front of the door at the top of the stairs

to the second floor, Harvey re-locked the door, removed his homemade lock pick, then got up and slowly went down the stairs back to his dormitory on the first floor, making sure nobody saw him, or so he thought.

He had got up early that morning in order to try the lock when he knew everyone else would be getting up and getting ready for the new day.

Going back into the dormitory, he went to his cupboard and opened his rucksack. Feeling for the hidden flap, which he had made to create a false bottom, he returned the lock pick to its hiding place, where it joined the tools and other lock picks that he had made. He closed his cupboard, went to the bathroom, and then joined the other boys to go downstairs for breakfast. When this was finished, the children gathered in the classroom.

"To begin our class today," began Miss Stratton, "I think it is proper that you should all know something about of the name of our Foundation. Saint Ettie." She paused and gave herself a stern, mental ticking-off, "Saint Etheldreda," she continued, noticing that Emily had turned red, "was the third daughter of an English king when England had lots of little kingdoms. She was born over one thousand three hundred years ago, in the year AD 636 to be exact, and she lived until she was around forty years old. Although she was a king's daughter and could have lived in luxury, she preferred a simple life and wanted to be a nun. Her father would not allow this and demanded that she marry. Her first husband died but, at her father's insistence, she married again.

"Eventually, she did become a nun, and she built a monastery on her lands at a place called Ely. Saint Etheldreda dedicated her life to helping others and always put other people before herself. Many wonderful things happened to her. While she was travelling on a very hot day, she became tired. She stuck the stick she used to help her walk, into the ground, sat down and rested. When she woke up, the stick had grown leaves and branches, which gave her shade. It later grew into a huge oak tree. After she died more miracles happened in her name. So that's Saint Etheldreda," concluded Miss Stratton. "At least you now know a little bit about her. Now," she continued, "today we will have the following lessons." The children listened as she explained the schedule of learning for the day.

Miss Stratton was beginning to get to know the children. After dinner that evening, when sitting in their private sitting room, Miss Stratton discussed a problem that she could see coming with Mrs Hutchins and Miss Marigold.

"What do you think of Brendon, Mrs Hutchins?" she asked.

"Well," replied Mrs Hutchins. "He seems a steady boy, not stupid. I think he looks out for the younger ones as well."

"What do you think, Miss Marigold?" said Miss Stratton, turning to her assistant."

"I agree with Mrs Hutchins," she replied. "He seems very responsible and quite mature for his age."

Miss Stratton discussed her problem with the two ladies and quite quickly they came to a decision that they were all happy with. Taking the first opportunity that came along, Miss Stratton asked Brandon to come with her to her office.

"Don't look so worried, Brandon," said Miss Stratton, smiling, as she saw the look of caution and nervousness appear on his face. "You have not done anything wrong." They entered her office and she asked him to close the door and sit down.

"Brandon," she began, "you are sixteen years old and the oldest of the children here. After some very serious thought about our present situation, I have decided to ask your assistance. I am asking because I cannot make you do it, and

I would not wish to anyway. We have limited staff here, only the three of us at the moment, and it is not possible for us to carry out our duties inside this building as well as being outside. We believe that it is not only your right to be allowed outside in the evenings when it is light and on the weekends, but that it would be of great benefit to us all. Once a school has been arranged for you all, then things will be a bit different, but we have not managed to do that yet. What I want, Brandon, is for you to take charge of the children when they are outside, when no member of staff is present. It is a great responsibility, and I do not ask it lightly. It is not always easy to keep an eye on so many, especially as there is a mix of boys and girls, some of whom are still quite young. So, what do you think? Will you help us, Brandon?"

A deep feeling of accomplishment gripped him. This was a rite of passage. He was now being treated as an adult, able to make his own decisions. People were placing their trust in him. and he was proud but also humbled. He understood what was being asked of him and his respect for Miss Stratton became intense.

"Yes Miss. I would love to do that. I'll try not to let you down."

"I know you won't, Brandon," replied Miss Stratton with a smile. "And thank you for your help. Just one thing," she continued. "I know I don't really have to say this because you will anyway, but whatever happens, always be straight and truthful with me, and no matter what, everything will be OK." Standing up, she put out her hand, which Brandon took, and they shook hands.

The children had got up early. Brandon had told them what had been said in Miss Stratton's office and they were going to go out for the day. Throwing open the curtains, Rachael uttered a cry of dismay.

"It's raining," she said with huge disappointment. The other girls peered through the window.

"We can't go out in that," said Evie. "We would get soaked."

Meeting up with the boys in the dining room for breakfast, the girls asked Brandon what they were going to do now that they could not go out.

"There's not much we can do," he replied. "We will just have to stay indoors, maybe read a book, or play some games."

Let down and somehow cheated, the children went to the TV room after they had finished eating. Jake and Freya started reading books, which was a pastime they enjoyed. The others started to play cards and board games, but after a while they became very bored. With nothing to really occupy their minds or interest them, the more energetic personalities, especially Grace and Alexander, began looking for trouble. Grace started to needle Jake that he always had his nose in a book and Jasmine egged her on. Alexander joined in and told Faith she was always sulking. Brandon told them to stop it but he was ignored. Freya then sprang to Jake's defence and told Jasmine she was stupid. Zac told Freya that she was as bad as Jake. The bickering got worse and worse. Then, Emily started to whistle her little tune, but after the first note Max immediately shouted at her to shut up. Emily burst into tears so Rachael shouted at everyone to leave her alone. The situation was getting totally out of hand.

"Enough!" shouted Brandon. "I'm fed up with this. If you don't stop all the arguing I'm going to get Miss Stratton." This produced the desired effect, and the atmosphere in the room cooled. Brandon picked up the car magazine he had found during their last visit to the park and said he was going upstairs to read it in peace. Max said he would join him. The others all looked around for something to do. Most of them tried to find a book to read. Then Rachael spoke.

"Harvey," said Rachael. "Have you been up to the top floors?" She knew he had because she had seen him coming down, but he had not seen her.

"Why do you want to know?" asked Harvey with a wary voice.

"Oh, I don't know," she replied. "Maybe look around up there for something to do."

"We shouldn't go up there," said Jake.

"Why not?" said Rachael. "Nobody said we couldn't."

"Nobody except us knows what Harvey can do," said Alexander, "especially with locked doors."

"Oh, come on Harvey," insisted Rachael. "I'll give you a kiss if you do it," and she teased him by pouting her lips. Harvey looked down shyly his cheeks turning red.

"Ah shut up, Rachael," he muttered.

Grace, Evie, Freya and Jasmine all started giggling and making eyes at Harvey, making him uncomfortable.

"We would have to have a lookout," said Zac, "in case Miss Stratton or Miss Marigold come upstairs."

"There's not much point in that," said Jake. We can't come down fast enough. They will see the open doors and catch us up there."

"You're all scaredy cats," said Grace. "I'd go on my own if I could open the doors."

Jasmine, Alexander and Zac, not wanting Grace to show them up, agreed to go up as well. Then Emily said she wanted to go too.

"Come on Harvey," said Rachael. "Go and get your things. Show us how brave you are."

"OK, OK," Harvey said with reluctance. "You all stay here for a minute," and he left to go to his dormitory. He returned a few minutes later, and very quietly, the children began making their way to the second floor.

"Good job Brandon isn't here," whispered Rachael to

nobody in particular. "Now he's a bit in charge of us, he would probably try to stop us."

"We better take our shoes off so they can't hear us walking around," said Freya.

"Good idea," said Jake. "We had better not talk, or only talk in whispers," he added. Grace said she would hold Harvey's shoes even though they were probably smelly.

Kneeling in front of the door, Harvey put his lock pick into the lock and, because he had opened this door before, it did not take him long before they were all standing in the corridor. They counted a total of nine doors along the corridor and Rachael promised Harvey two kisses if he would open them all. She pouted her lips again in an exaggerated manner. Harvey shot her a scornful, withering look. As they were all the same design of lock as the first door at the top of the stairs, Harvey quickly opened the doors to all the rooms. The first door they opened was a small bathroom. The next seven rooms, six small and one quite large, were all empty, and the last door was another small bathroom. After looking out of the windows in the empty rooms to see what they could see of the street below, the children quickly lost interest.

"Let's go to the top one," whispered Grace.

Harvey's skills soon had the children standing in the big room on the third floor. As the room was empty, they could easily see the other door at the back of the room, and after Harvey opened it, they found themselves in another small corridor. The four storage-room doors beckoned. The first storage room they went into had some small boxes on a shelf containing little packets of coiled wire and other items, but none of the children knew what they were. The next two storage rooms were empty.

"I'm getting a bit fed up with this," said Harvey. "There's nothing much to see and all these locks are the same. There's no fun in it."

"Oh, go on Harvey," said Emily. "There's only one more door anyway so you may as well open it. Then we will know for sure if there is anything there."

Sighing, Harvey knelt before the door, and within seconds, they all heard the lock spring open. He got up and Jasmine squeezed in front of him. She turned the handle and slowly opened the door.

Chapter 8

"Wow," exclaimed Jasmine, "there's something in here."

Harvey, Rachael and Alexander squeezed into the room with Jasmine, and the others peered in from the doorway as best they could. The light was dim, but they could easily make out most of the shapes.

"They're instruments," said Rachael in breathless excitement. "Violins and things."

Jostling each other to better see into the room, the children in the corridor stretched their necks and moved their heads around so their wide, excited eyes could see what treasures they had found.

"Look, over there, there are some drums," said Zac, pointing his finger towards the darkest corner. "And there's a trumpet as well," he added.

Carefully moving around, the children tried to see all the instruments in the room.

"Wouldn't it be great if we could play these things?" exclaimed Evie.

"It takes a long time to be able to play an instrument properly," answered Harvey, "and lots of practice."

"Well, we could try," said Faith. "It would be something to do and may be fun."

"How do we tell Miss Stratton about this? We are not supposed to be up here," said Jake.

"She'll want to know how we got here in the first place, which is going to get me into trouble," said Harvey. "I don't want Miss Stratton getting mad at me."

The children fell silent, twisting their lips in thought.

"Let's think about it," said Jasmine.

"There must be some way," echoed Grace. "There has to be."

*   *   *

"Where are they?" said Brandon to Max. He was worried and the responsibility Miss Stratton had placed on his shoulders was making him nervous.

"They're not in the TV room, nor in the dormitories, and they won't be in the kitchen," said Max. "They must be upstairs somewhere," he continued. "Maybe they have persuaded Harvey to open some doors."

"I hope not," said Brandon. "Miss Stratton would give me hell, especially as she wants me to look after everyone when we go outside." The thought that they were doing something that would make him lose face in Miss Stratton's eyes made him angry.

"We had better go and check, and fast," said Brandon.

The two boys went quickly and as quietly as they could to the second floor, but they found the door was locked. They continued up the next flight of stairs to the top floor. The door was open. Brandon and Max cautiously entered the large, empty room. They saw that the door on the other side of the room was open and, as they approached it, they heard low murmuring voices. Walking quietly, they peered through the door and saw some of their friends standing around at the end of the corridor. Brandon coughed.

Whirling around like spinning tops, scared faces and shocked eyes locked onto Brandon in an instant.

"Brandon," hissed Freya, the look of fear on her face changing to one of annoyance. "You scared me to death."

"What are you doing here?" growled Brandon in a low, angry voice. "Miss Stratton will get really mad at me if she finds out you are up here. I'm supposed to be responsible for you now. How do you think this is going to make me look if we get found out?" His anger was tangible, and the children took on a shamefaced look.

"Sorry Brandon," said Evie. "We didn't think about

56

that. Please don't be mad. Anyway, look what we've found, Brandon," she continued. "Instruments."

The children in the corridor moved so that Brandon could look inside the room. He told Rachael and Alexander to give him some space so he could take a better look.

Quickly scanning the room and getting an idea of what was in there, he turned and walked back into the corridor. "Not sure we can do anything with that stuff," he said brusquely. "Anyway, we are going back downstairs now before Miss Stratton catches us."

Leaving the room, he told his friends to get back to the TV room as quickly and as quietly as they could and told Harvey to make sure he locked all the doors properly.

When they were all safely back in the TV room, Brandon let out a huge sigh of relief.

"Never do that to me again," he said. "I don't need a heart attack."

"We have to find a way to tell Miss Stratton about this without getting ourselves into trouble, especially Harvey," said Faith. "I would love to be able to play one of those instruments, I really, really would."

"Funny, but I always wanted to play a trumpet," said Zac. "Then I could blow it in your ear Jake," he added with a laugh.

"Sorry, but there is no way I am ever going to tell Miss Stratton about this. She won't trust me anymore and I don't want that to happen," Brandon said.

"Maybe if you could persuade her it would be good for us, Brandon, she won't get so mad," said Emily. The other children looked at Emily in amazement.

"That is a truly great idea, Emily," said Jake, looking at her with new eyes.

Emily's face changed into a portrait of euphoria. She began to feel something that she had not felt for three years.

Something inside of her was returning. She could not say what but, she felt slightly more complete. She revelled in the attention.

"Yeah," said Grace, grasping this solution with great enthusiasm. "That may be a way to do it. She wants us to be happy, so maybe she won't get so angry with us."

They all looked at Brandon. He remained silent; his face set in a grim expression. He was not happy at all. "I'm still not going to do it," he said. The silence that followed his statement was tense. Grace stared at Brandon, her face chipped from granite, her eyes adamant and unblinking, and her lips compressed so tight they had almost disappeared. Then, in a voice of unbending determination, she said, "Brandon, if you don't even try to do this for us, then every time we go out somewhere, I'm gonna make your life hell."

"That's blackmail," retorted Brandon angrily.

"You've got it, Brandon," Grace replied.

Harvey groaned.

His stomach churned, his nerves were screaming, and his knees were clamped tightly together. Brandon sat opposite Miss Stratton in her office. He dug his fingernails into the palms of his hands, his mind racing to find the words he needed.

"So, Brandon. What can I do for you?" Miss Stratton asked. She noticed that he looked uncomfortable.

"I'm very sorry to trouble you, Miss," began Brandon, "but could I talk to you about something?"

"Of course," replied Miss Stratton.

He was not sure how to begin. "We have been talking a bit between ourselves," he started, "and we've thought of something we could all do together, like a hobby." He paused.

"Go on Brandon," said Miss Stratton.

"Well," he continued, "we thought about playing musical instruments together."

Miss Stratton's eyebrows nearly launched into space. "Really, Brandon?" she said with great surprise. "I did not know you were all musically minded. Well," she continued, her eyebrows having made it back to earth, "it's a lovely idea but I'm afraid that would be difficult. Musical instruments are expensive and I do not have the money for it. If I had, I would certainly give your idea some serious consideration."

Brandon swallowed hard and continued. "Well actually, Miss," and he braced himself for the firing squad, we maybe don't have to buy any."

"How do you mean, Brandon?" Miss Stratton asked with sharp curiosity.

Hoping that his shirt was not becoming too wet with his sweat, he answered, "Maybe there are some already here, Miss."

"What are you not telling me, Brandon?" demanded Miss Stratton. "Where are these instruments? The truth please."

Brandon knew that he had to be straight with her. "On the third floor, Miss," he replied. He felt sick.

"The third floor," said Miss Stratton loudly. "And how did you get up to the third floor?" she asked in a hard, interrogating voice. She now understood his nervousness.

"Harvey," Brandon replied, hoping that Harvey would understand this letting down of a friend and could forgive him for it.

"Harvey," queried Miss Stratton. "What did Harvey do?"

"He opened the doors, Miss," replied Brandon.

"How?" demanded Miss Stratton.

"He has a thing about locks, Miss," mumbled Brandon.

"Explain," said Miss Stratton, "and all of it please."

In order to protect his friend as much as possible, Brandon continued, "Harvey loves locks, Miss. He's not interested in going into rooms or anything like that. He doesn't do it to pry or to steal anything, he just loves locks. He opens them and more or less just locks them again straight away."

Brandon was digging his fingernails into his hands as hard as he could. He was scared stiff of what was going to happen now.

Miss Stratton was silent. She fixed Brandon with her searching grey eyes and, deciding that at least Brandon was being straight with her, which actually made her quite happy, she let out a long, slow breath. Her first reaction to give Harvey the worst telling off he would ever have in his life had subsided.

"How does Harvey open the locks?" she asked with curiosity.

"He has some bent wires and other things," said Brandon, "but he never shows them to anybody. I don't know where he keeps them because I've never asked. Harvey keeps all that stuff and how he does it to himself," he finished, his eyes looking down at the desk.

"I see," said Miss Stratton. "You had better show me Brandon, and no, do not call Harvey. We will do this with our proper keys." She got up, opened her office door and went to Miss Marigold's office. Her door was open, so Miss Stratton asked her for the keys to the upstairs doors. Handing the keys to Miss Stratton, Miss Marigold enquired if everything was OK.

"I hope so, Miss Marigold. I just have to go and take a look at something." Miss Stratton paused. "Actually," she continued, "it would be a good idea if you would come with us."

Miss Stratton, Miss Marigold and Brandon went up to the third floor.

The door had closed, the footsteps had gone away and the silence returned. The instruments let go of their pent-up breath in a great whoosh of relief.

"Well," drawled Charles, "to parody some words of a famous man, this is either the end of the beginning or the beginning of the end. Let's hope it is the former."

"Well, I for one, am glad that somebody found us," said Vivianne. "At least something will happen, hopefully good, but if not, so be it. Anything is better than being here for years and years until most of us crumble away into dust."

"OK," continued Veronica. "Are we all agreed that if and when anyone comes back, and if they take us someplace else, we all keep quiet until we can figure out which way the wind's blowing? No offence Theodore, Teddy and Charles?" she added quickly.

The instruments knew that Veronica believed in the myth that it was possible for people to hear them talk. The rest of them didn't, but they agreed to do as she asked to humour her.

"Very wise," said Charles. "Best to watch and wait until we know more."

He had no sooner finished talking when they heard new footsteps approaching. They heard a key being inserted into the lock, the key turned, the lock clunked, and the door opened again.

"Well, well," murmured Miss Stratton, after taking a brief look around. "Aladdin's Cave." She turned to Miss Marigold.

"Do you know anything about violins or any other instruments, Miss Marigold?" she asked.

"I'm afraid not, Miss Stratton," replied Miss Marigold. "Sorry," she added.

"That's all right, Miss Marigold," replied Miss Stratton, laughing, "neither do I."

"Well, some things are obvious," Miss Stratton continued. "They all need a lot of cleaning for a start. There are some broken strings on at least two of the violins, oh, and that trombone does not look too healthy either."

Miss Stratton turned to Brandon.

"So, you all want to play with these, do you?" It was more of a statement than a question, but Brandon nodded anyway.

Putting her organisational skills into action, Miss Stratton issued a string of instructions.

"Miss Marigold. Would you please go to the kitchen and tell Mrs Hutchins that we have some very dusty objects to bring downstairs and the only place I can think of at the moment is to put them on the dining room floor? Tell her I will be down shortly to explain. Brandon, go downstairs and get Max, Alexander, Harvey, Jake and Rachael to come up here. Tell all the others to go to the cupboard in the classroom, the one in the corner behind the blackboard, and take out plenty of old newspapers. Tell them to lay the papers on the floor. Ask Mrs Hutchins to show you the best place."

Brandon, looking very relieved that things seemed to be working out, ran down to tell his friends who were waiting anxiously in the TV room.

"What did she say?" asked Rachael, breathless and excited.

Smiling, Brandon raised his two hands with the thumbs up, and he relayed Miss Stratton's instructions to them. With eyes sparkling, the grinning children rushed off to their required destinations. Emily was skipping down the hall whistling her little tune as hard and as loud as she could.

The smaller instruments were laid out side-by-side on the floor. The larger ones, such as Celia the cello and Danny the double bass, stood against the dining room wall. Danny had nearly come to grief negotiating the stairs between the third and second floors and had only been saved by Max sticking his foot out to stop him sliding down the stairs like a whale on a water slide.

The only item still to be brought down was Dean, the drum kit. Brandon, Max and Jake, under instructions from Miss Stratton, were now busy with this operation. It had required some careful thought and investigation. They also had to borrow some tools from the small tool collection that Mrs Hutchins had, in order to dismantle Dean into manageable parts.

"My dear old hubby would have loved it," Mrs Hutchins exclaimed. "When he died, I could not bear to part with his tools. I bought some of them for him for birthdays, so they are very sentimental to me."

With great care and taking their time, they moved Dean down to the dining room with only minor damage to the paintwork on the walls, which made Miss Stratton wince, but she did not tell them off. It was a hard enough job as it was.

Once all the instruments had been brought to the dining room, an anxious thought came into Miss Stratton's head. How many instruments were there? She began to count them. When she counted the last instrument, which happened to be the drum kit, she felt elated. Thirteen. She breathed and let out a grateful sigh. "OK," said Miss Stratton, "let's have a good look."

Three of the violins had broken strings, one guitar also had a broken string, and the other had a big chip out of the enamel work, which was a pity. The cello and the double bass looked intact. The trumpet looked OK, but the trombone had an odd bend in it, and also a large dent in its horn. The metal bits down the length of the clarinet were hanging off at strange angles, but nobody was sure if this was how it was supposed to be or not.

"Miss Stratton," cried Freya, "there is a book in the TV room about musical instruments." Turning to Jake she continued, "Have you seen it too, Jake?" After a moment his eyes brightened. "Yeah, the tall thin book on the top shelf at the end," he said.

"Yes," said Freya, "it's too big to fit on the lower shelves so it's at the top. Shall I get it Miss?" she asked.

"I think it would be better if we looked at the book in the TV room," replied Miss Stratton. "It may get dirty if we bring it in here."

They all made their way to the TV room.

"Things are looking up," murmured Verity.

"Shush," hissed Veronica. "They may be back any minute."

As it was, it was a good fifteen minutes before everyone returned to the dining room. They had found the book and discovered that two violins had broken "E" strings, one violin had a broken "A" string, and the keys on the clarinet were, as Grace put it, "wonky". The drum kit could do with a bit of oil or something as some parts of it made a horrible squeaking noise.

Not too bad, thought Miss Stratton. Another thought occurred to her. "Did you find anything else in any of the other store rooms upstairs?" she asked.

The children hesitated slightly. "It's OK," said Miss Stratton, smiling. "I'm not going to get angry. I just want to know if maybe you found anything else up there that may help us fix these instruments."

"We found some boxes and tins in one of the other rooms," answered Rachael.

"Show me," said Miss Stratton. Rachael, Miss Marigold with her keys, and Miss Stratton went back to the third floor. They opened the door that Rachael pointed at and went in. There were two boxes and two tins which had already been opened.

"Let's take this stuff downstairs and see what we have," said Miss Stratton. "We will take it into the TV room and put it on some newspaper on the floor. Maybe we will find something in that music book that tells us what some of these things are."

With Rachael and Miss Marigold carrying the boxes and tins, they returned downstairs to the TV room. Fetching more newspapers from the classroom cupboard, they put the boxes and tins on the floor and began to take out all the things inside.

"OK," said Miss Stratton, "what have we got here?" It was not much.

There were five packets, each containing a coil of thin wire. Each packet had a label that said "E String". There were four orange lumps of some sort of resin, which the music book told them was "Rosin". This was used on the horsehair of the bows. The tin contained trumpet valve oil, but there was not much left in it, and the nearly full pot had some sort of grease in it. The bulk of the things in the boxes were a whole assortment of rags.

Miss Stratton, Miss Marigold and Rachael, rejoined the others in the dining room.

"It would seem that the first thing that needs to be done," Miss Stratton said to the children, "is that everything needs a bit of a clean, just to get rid of the dust and cobwebs. Now, what can we use?"

"The cleaners have some stuff in their cupboard in the hall," said Faith. "Couldn't we borrow something from there?"

"We don't have a key to that cupboard," answered Miss Stratton, and without pausing, she fixed Harvey with what she tried to make a stern look but failed, and said, "Don't even think about it, Harvey."

Harvey, who had been anxiously waiting for Miss Stratton to tell him to come to her office, smiled sheepishly, but with enormous relief. The comment, given with the breaking smile that Miss Stratton had tried to hide, told Harvey that he might very well be "off the hook" with his lock picking activities.

With a sigh, knowing that she was going to disappoint them, Miss Stratton said sadly, "Sorry kids, the cleaning will have to wait until tomorrow." Then, in a flash of inspiration to relieve the disappointment, Miss Stratton said that they would go out tomorrow and buy some proper dusters and cleaning equipment to clean the instruments, instead of having lessons.

There was a collective cheer from the children who obviously thought this was a great idea.

Going into the dining room, Mrs Hutchins saw all the instruments on the floor and leaning against the walls. She studied them for a few moments before approaching Miss Stratton. "What an amazing find!" she exclaimed. "Who would have thought that these would have been left behind from the old music school? How did you find them?"

Miss Stratton explained, giving all the details as she did not want Mrs Hutchins to feel in anyway left out. Returning her gaze to the violins on the floor, Mrs Hutchins remarked that they looked awfully fragile. Miss Stratton agreed but said there wasn't really anywhere else to put them. Slowly rubbing her chin and glancing back and forth, Mrs Hutchins made a suggestion.

"In my experience," she began, "things left on floors tend to get damaged no matter how careful you try to be.

Maybe we could find some blankets or something to put on the table and then we could put them out of harm's way."

"I take your point, Mrs Hutchins," replied Miss Stratton. "They would be safer on the table, but then where would we eat?"

"We could all eat in the kitchen," replied Mrs Hutchins. "The table's plenty big enough. We only need to bring the chairs in from the dining room, provided they're clean, of course," she added.

"Are you sure you don't mind Mrs Hutchins? It would be an easy solution," replied Miss Stratton.

"No problem at all," replied Mrs Hutchins with a laugh. "It would save me having to carry everything in here each mealtime."

Miss Stratton could not sleep. As she lay in her bed, the doubts started to creep into her mind. What was she doing? Was it the right thing? Cleaning the instruments was one thing, but what about repairs, tuning them and, how exactly were the children going to learn to play them? Maybe she had been a bit hasty in allowing it to get as far as it had already. Maybe she should have been firmer and said no to the whole idea, even though it would have been a great disappointment for the children. Miss Stratton tossed and turned, trying to grapple with all of these questions. She eventually fell into a few hours of restless sleep.

She woke feeling tired and troubled. At eight o'clock she went to the girls' dormitory and knocked on the door to wake them up. She returned to her sitting room and sat down, but she could not keep still. Fidgeting with nervous tension, she got up and wandered back into the corridor. Ambling along the corridor without any focus on what she was doing, she wandered back into the girls' dormitory and looked out of the window. All the girls were in their bathroom getting ready for the day. Turning to leave the room, the bolt of electrifying energy slammed into her. The words on the poster above the door hit her like a hard slap in the face. For a moment she stood stock still, and then she connected to a vast reservoir of vitality and her body soaked up every last drop of it. It surged and crackled through every fibre of her being. She was charged; she was strong; she was ready, and she was invincible.

Striding down to her office, she sat down at her desk and marshalled her talents together into a formidable army. Picking up her pen and taking a piece of paper, she started to plan her campaign. She already knew she needed cleaning equipment. It would also be good to have some covers or boxes to keep the instruments in so that they were kept clean and protected. Next, she had to find out the condition of the instruments, the cost of repairs and spare parts, getting them tuned, and finally, the biggest hurdle she faced, teaching the children how to play them.

She made some notes on her pad and then reached for the telephone directory and, carefully reading the small print, she found what she was looking for.

The Music Shop was in the middle of the city, in the new shopping complex. It was too far away to walk, so they would have to take the bus. Opening a locked drawer in her desk, and wondering with a smile on her face if Harvey could open it with his lock picks, she took out a metal cash box. She checked the amount of money she had and saw there was enough inside to pay for the bus fares with plenty over to pay for cleaning equipment. She closed the cash box and re-locked the drawer. Looking at her watch, she saw it was fifteen minutes to nine. She hurried to the kitchen where she found Mrs Hutchins and Miss Marigold having a cup of tea.

"Good morning, ladies," said Miss Stratton brightly.

"Good morning, Miss Stratton," they replied.

"Would you like some tea?" asked Mrs Hutchins.

"Oh, yes please," replied Miss Stratton, "that would be lovely. There is something I would like to talk to you about ladies," she continued and, after seating herself at the kitchen table, she explained her plans to them.

"I know the children will technically be missing classes today," she concluded, "but, in a way, this is educating them, but in a more practical manner."

"You can't beat practical experience," stated Mrs Hutchins, "no matter what the subject."

The children went down for breakfast as usual, and then they gathered in the classroom. Miss Stratton entered the room and went up to her desk.

"Well," she began. "As I said yesterday afternoon, today we will carry on with our music project. We will go into the city and buy some cleaning equipment and other things that we will need to keep the instruments clean and safe." The children hung on her every word.

"To begin with," Miss Stratton continued, "as well as cleaning materials, we will need covers or storage boxes for the instruments. Miss Marigold and Mrs Hutchins will take some of you to look for suitable material to make covers. Mrs Hutchins tells me that she knows her way around a sewing machine, so she will be able to make the covers for us. I'm not so sure about the storage boxes. Does anyone have any ideas?"

"Maybe I know somewhere," said Max. He explained about the second-hand luggage shop he knew and Miss Stratton immediately congratulated Max for such a good idea. So, it was arranged. Miss Marigold would take the boys to the second-hand luggage shop and Mrs Hutchins would take Rachael, Evie, Freya and Faith to look for cover material. Miss Stratton would take Jasmine, Emily and Grace to the Music Shop to get the proper cleaning equipment for the instruments.

"So," said Miss Stratton, "off you go and get your coats and be back in the hall as quickly as you can." Harvey was the last to leave the boys' dormitory and go back down the stairs. His fingers felt the lock pick and piece of wire which were in his pocket. Harvey liked to be prepared.

About ten minutes later, Miss Stratton and Mrs Hutchins, together with their groups, left Saint Etheldreda's, and walked towards the bus stop. Miss Marigold, with the boys, went in the opposite direction, as the second-hand luggage shop was not in the centre of the city, but more on the outskirts. It was not so far away and, all being young, they had decided to walk.

Arriving at the central bus station, Miss Stratton and Mrs Hutchins guided the children to the shopping complex. Studying a plan which showed where all the shops were located, Mrs Hutchins took her group off to a large department store which had a big fabric department. Before they split up, they agreed to be back at the starting point by the shop plan at twelve o'clock. Miss Stratton took Jasmine, Grace and Emily, and after a five-minute walk, they stood in front of the Music Shop.

"Wow, look at them," cried Jasmine with excitement, as she pointed to a beautiful display of shining musical instruments in the big shop window. Feeling a little daunted, Miss Stratton hesitated, but with the girls tugging at her hands, they soon found themselves inside. The shop widened out inside and stretched back for some distance. It was quite a large area.

Scanning some of the shelves around her, Miss Stratton started searching for anything that looked like cleaning equipment such as dusters, but she did not see anything. She began walking down the aisles of the busy shop, searching left and right. A young woman was standing looking through the shop's display of records, and she glanced at the tall, grey-haired lady and the three girls as they passed. Miss Stratton looked for a shop assistant, and although she could see quite a lot of them, they all appeared busy with other customers. Miss Stratton did not want to interrupt any of them with a question about dusters, so she continued with the children, walking up and down all the aisles, but without success.

After about twenty minutes, they were more or less back where they started, and once again they passed the young woman at the records display.

"Maybe she knows," blurted out Grace loudly to Miss Stratton as they approached the young woman. The young woman looked up and smiled at the children and Miss Stratton who, looking embarrassed, told Grace to pipe down. Miss Stratton returned the smile and was just about to move on when the young woman spoke.

"Are you looking for something in particular?" she asked.

"Well, actually, we are trying to find some cleaning materials like dusters and brushes for cleaning musical instruments," said Miss Stratton, a little bit flustered, "but we have not seen anything like that so far."

"Oh," said the young woman, "they are over here." She lead Miss Stratton and the children to a small recess in one of the corners of the shop that Miss Stratton and the children had missed during their wandering. She pointed at the shelves with cloths, dusters, all shapes and sizes of brushes and a whole assortment of tins and pots.

"Thank you ever so much," said Miss Stratton with genuine gratitude.

"My pleasure ma'am," replied the young woman with a wide, bright smile. She looked down at the children, the smallest of whom was whistling.

"Please stop whistling, Emily," said Miss Stratton in a gentle tone. "I wish I could find out the name of the tune you keep whistling. Then maybe we could get a record or something so that you could learn and whistle all of it instead of the little bit you remember."

The young woman, who had not yet started to move away, replied.

"It's the *Holberg Suite*, ma'am, or, should I say the *Prelude to the Holberg Suite*. It was written by a composer named Grieg." It was one of the young woman's favourite pieces, which is why she had been able to recognise it so quickly from only hearing a few bars. She saw the rather blank expression on Miss Stratton's face.

"Wait," the young woman continued, "I'll write it down for you." She quickly rummaged in her handbag and produced a slightly crumpled piece of paper, which was an unimportant sales leaflet from a magazine she subscribed to, and wrote down the name of the piece. Her handwriting was not up to its usual standard, as she had nothing hard to write on, so the composer's name came out as "Greg" instead of "Grieg". She handed the piece of paper to Miss Stratton who once again thanked the young woman with sincere warmth.

"You are very welcome," replied the young lady, and she moved off to continue looking at the records.

"There Emily," said Miss Stratton. "Maybe now you can learn the whole thing if we can get a record of it or something."

By twelve o'clock, Miss Stratton, Jasmine, Emily and Grace returned to the starting point by the shop plan carrying two bags from the Music Shop, full of bright yellow dusters and a collection of brushes. Miss Stratton had looked at all the pots and tins but, being completely ignorant of the different types of oils and greases and all the other unknown contents in these items, plus the fact that most of them were quite expensive, she had not purchased any of them, but just stuck with the dusters and brushes.

A few moments later, Mrs Hutchins appeared with some rather large packages.

"We found some good material," she said, beaming to Miss Stratton, "and what's more, nearly all of it was at sale price; all end of the roll items. It will do very well for what we want." They walked back to the bus station and took the next bus back to Saint Etheldreda's.

An hour later, Miss Stratton was getting worried. She peered out of the window of her sitting room and scanned the street, but the only thing she saw were the usual cars and an old truck that had seen much better days coming down the street. She was about to sit down again when the old truck stopped in front of the Foundation. The truck door opened and Miss Stratton's eyes opened wide with utter astonishment as Miss Marigold climbed out of the cab. She ran quickly to the front door and flung it open to meet Miss Marigold at the top of the steps.

"Miss Marigold!" exclaimed Miss Stratton. "Is everything alright? What are you doing in that old truck and why is it still parked there and where are the boys?"

"Oh, Miss Stratton," replied Miss Marigold, her eyes sparkling and her face glowing with excitement, "the boys are fine. They are in the back of the truck."

"Oh, OK," said Miss Stratton, relieved that there were no problems. "Well, get the boys out quickly please, Miss Marigold, and then come and tell me all about it," she said much more calmly.

The truck driver had already opened the back doors of

the truck while Miss Stratton and Miss Marigold were talking, and the boys bounded up the steps all looking very pleased with themselves.

"So Miss Marigold, what's all this about?" asked Miss Stratton, full of curiosity.

"Boxes for the instruments, Miss Stratton," said Miss Marigold. "We have some terrific boxes to keep them in and they were free." The truck driver and his companion came up the steps.

"Could you tell us what to do with the boxes please ma'am?" asked the driver. "We cannot stay here too long or we might get a parking ticket."

"Please bring them in and put them in the classroom," said Miss Stratton, smiling. "Miss Marigold, please show these gentlemen the way."

The driver and his companion returned to the truck and started to carry inside the blue boxes of various sizes, which they stacked on the floor. It took five trips to do this as there were ten boxes in all and they had to move some tables and chairs to get everything in.

"Thanks guys," Miss Marigold said to the driver and his companion. "We really appreciate all your help. It was kind of you to help us." She gave them a dazzling smile.

"Pleasure ma'am," replied the driver and, as the truck pulled away, he blew Miss Marigold a kiss.

Miss Marigold's fingertips flew to her cheeks as she watched him drive away.

Seated in the TV room, Miss Stratton waited to hear what had happened. Miss Marigold began to explain.

"It was all down to Harvey really," she said. "We told the shopkeeper at the luggage shop what we were looking for and he said he might have something suitable in his shed at the back of the shop. That's where we found the blue boxes. There was also a beautiful set of suitcases in the shed, so I asked the shopkeeper why such lovely items were in the shed and not in the shop. He said he could not sell them because they were locked and he did not have the keys. I asked him, if we could open the cases, could he give us a good deal on the blue boxes? He said that if we could open the cases, we could have the boxes for free and he would deliver them for free as well. Harvey did the rest," Miss Marigold concluded.

"Well Harvey, you seem to be making a name for yourself," said Miss Stratton, trying to give her words the warmth she felt, but at the same time conveying the message that he had better keep on the straight and narrow. She made a mental note that she had better find a local locksmith where Harvey could practice his passions legally. She would never forgive herself if he became a safe-cracker. Harvey smiled shyly, but proudly, and Miss Stratton smiled back.

Miss Stratton rapidly reported on her morning's purchases at the Music Shop and ended by saying, "Oh, and we found out the name of the piece of music that Emily keeps whistling."

"How did you do that?" asked Miss Marigold.

"The young woman I just told you about," replied Miss Stratton. "The lady who showed us where the dusters and brushes were. She heard Emily whistling and she came right out with the name of it. She even wrote it on a piece of paper for us. Wait a minute, I'll get it from my office." Going quickly to her office, Miss Stratton took the piece of paper from her handbag and returned to the TV room.

"It's called the *Prelude to the Holberg Suite* by somebody called 'Greg'."

"How extraordinary," said Miss Marigold. "Fancy finding that out."

Miss Stratton glanced briefly at the back of the piece of

paper and noted that it was some sort of advertisement from a magazine and she also noticed the name and address of a person in the top left-hand corner. She folded the piece of paper and put it in her cardigan pocket.

Mrs Hutchins, who had been sitting listening to Miss Stratton and Miss Marigold, chipped in, "Well, that's nice for you, Emily. You can learn the rest of your tune now you know what it is." She then continued to tell everyone about the materials she had obtained from the big department store. "We will have to do some measuring up, and then try to make some patterns so that we can make the covers for the bigger instruments," Mrs Hutchins concluded.

"I have to hear the music first," Emily murmured, after Mrs Hutchins had finished speaking. "I can't whistle it unless it's in my head."

"We will have to see what we can do about that," said Miss Stratton with understanding tenderness, "but for now, first things first." She glanced at her watch and was surprised to see that it was nearly five o'clock. "Oh my, look how late it is," she said.

"I'll get the oven on now," said Mrs Hutchins. "We can eat in about forty-five minutes.

"OK everyone," said Miss Stratton. "Let's all get cleaned up and get ready for dinner."

Miss Stratton went to her office. She took out her list of jobs to do for the project and began adding to it. She would ask the cleaners to hoover out the boxes the following morning, and also ask them if, at some point, they could clean the rooms on the second and third floors. They would need somewhere to keep the instruments safely and also somewhere where the children could get down to the hard part of learning to play them. She did not want to use the classroom for this purpose as she was afraid the noise so close to her office would drive her and Miss Marigold crazy.

At this point in time, Miss Stratton had absolutely no idea how she was going to achieve some of these things, especially how the children would learn to play the instruments. They would also need some chairs to sit on unless the situation with finding a school was sorted out soon. If that happened, then they could use the chairs and tables from the classroom. Getting up, she left her office and went to the kitchen.

Dinner was lively with experiences shared about the day out at the shopping complex, and after the usual washing up and other chores had been done, they all moved into the dining room.

"OK, here's the plan," said Miss Stratton, as if addressing her troops. "Brandon and Max, you start cleaning the guitars. Harvey, Alexander and Jake, you take the big double bass and the clarinet. Jasmine and Faith, you clean the cello. Zac, you can clean the trumpet and the trombone. Rachael, you take Grace and Freya and make a start on the violins. Evie, you can help Mrs Hutchins with measuring all the instruments so that she can start making the patterns for the covers. Miss Marigold and I will help you with that once everybody has started. Emily, you can do the drums."

"I don't want to do the drums," said Emily in a sullen voice.

"Emily," said Miss Stratton, with patience, "some of these instruments are quite big and heavy. You don't have to lift or move anything with the drums, so it will be easier for you."

"I want to do the violins with Rachael," repeated Emily. "I don't want to clean those stupid drums."

"Emily," replied Miss Stratton firmly, "please don't be difficult. You will please do as I ask."

Emily stared defiantly at Miss Stratton for a moment with eyes glaring, nostrils flared, lips quivering, her whole body shaking with fury. Then she turned, ran to the drums, picked up a drumstick, and with all her strength brought it crashing down on the big brass cymbal. Everyone froze as the great crescendo of vibrating, shimmering sound bounced around the room. Slowly, the walls of the room soaked up the sound and there was silence. Nobody moved.

"Oh, my dear, that's so much better. Just what I needed. My sinuses feel better already. Thank you so much. Oh, sorry Veronica, I think I've put my foot in it again," came the strong, cultured voice from Camilla, the big brass cymbal.

Emily screamed.

Chapter 9

"It talked," screamed Emily, "it talked!"

She sat on Miss Marigold's lap, shaking with fear after she had rushed away from the drums and flung herself into Miss Marigold arms. Miss Marigold, completely startled, wrapped her arms around Emily in a maternal, protective hug.

"Calm down, Emily," she said, even though calm was not what Miss Marigold was feeling herself at that moment. "Whatever's the matter?" she continued. "Did the loud noise frighten you?"

"It talked," cried out Emily again.

"What talked?" asked Miss Marigold in a soothing tone.

"That big yellowy plate on the stick," continued Emily, her little shoulders still heaving.

"The cymbal talked?" said Miss Marigold, surprised.

"Yeah, that big plate; it talked," repeated Emily again.

Miss Marigold was no child psychiatrist, but she knew enough to know that it was best to agree with what children came out with sometimes, especially if they were obviously a bit frightened or upset. "OK," said Miss Marigold, "if you say it talked, I believe you."

"It did, it did!" repeated Emily.

"OK Emily, OK, just calm down. I don't think anything horrible is going to happen. Just relax and take some deep breaths," said Miss Marigold, trying to sooth and reassure the young girl.

Emily quietened down, released herself from Miss Marigold's arms and turned to see everyone else staring at her. She stared back, angry and sullen, and then Miss Stratton resumed command.

"Maybe we had better do this tomorrow," she said. "I think that you may be more tired than you think after today's day out. Go and watch a little TV and then go to bed. We will probably do a better job tomorrow anyway when we're all refreshed. There will be much better light as well," Miss Stratton concluded.

The children just nodded and filed out of the dining room and went to the TV room.

Once in the room, Emily, who hoped she had not upset her friends, said in a soft voice, "but I did hear a voice, I really did."

"I know," said Rachael, and after a little pause she added, "I thought I did, too."

"You heard her talk as well?" exclaimed Emily with a bright, surprised look.

"You really heard it, too. Honest? You're not just saying that?"

Rachael nodded. A moment later, she said to everyone in the room, "Put your hand up if you thought you heard some sort of voice." Rachael raised her hand; Emily raised her hand and then – so did everyone else.

"I nearly wet myself," said Grace, who then went bright red. "I didn't, but I nearly did," she added hastily, trying to cover her embarrassment.

"It was weird," said Zac.

"Wonder if it will happen again?" said Evie.

"I don't think the grown-ups heard it," chipped in Max.

"Well, I think it's scary," said Jasmine. "I don't want to think about it. Can we watch some TV please?"

They spent the rest of the evening reading or watching TV, but at some point, they all thought about the strange voice. Some began to doubt whether they had really heard it at all. They stayed watching TV for a little while before they drifted off to the dormitories and went to bed.

Emily lay on her back with her eyes wide open. The talking yellow plate filled her mind completely. It had frightened her when she first heard it in the dining room, but now, from the safety of her bed, it stirred unstoppable curiosity rather than fear. After a while, she could not hold herself back any more. She had to see if it was real.

She sat up, moved the covers to one side of the bed and slipped her legs out. Her feet touched the cool floor. She pushed herself up and reached for her dressing gown, which she slipped on with silent movements. Then she bent down and picked up her soft slippers. Looking around the room, she saw that her friends were all asleep, unmoving. The only sound was that of their steady breathing. Making no noise, she moved to the door and placed her hand on the door handle and held her breath as she slowly moved the handle down with great care, until, she cracked the door open. She stopped, and listened. Hearing no one call out, she opened the door further and moved out into the corridor. Pulling the door closed again, she relaxed her wrist and let the door handle return to its normal position of rest. She let go of her breath, and the warm air passed over her throat in a silent stream. She looked down the corridor. A small ray of moonlight shone through the window by the stairs, creating eerie shadows. Switching her slippers to her other hand, she stretched out her free arm and shuffled forward to touch the wall of the corridor. Emily began to tiptoe towards the moonlight, keeping her hand on the wall and sliding it forward as she moved in order to steady herself, inch by inch. The floor was cold on her toes and, after glancing back over her shoulder to check no one was creeping up behind her, she came to the top of the stairs. As soon as she could, she reached out, grasped the banister and turned to look down the stairs. She could feel her heart beating hard, and the moon cast her shadow down the staircase. Only the edges of the steps could be seen, and they led to the blackness below. She placed her right foot with great care onto the first step then followed this movement with her other foot. Her heart thumped faster as she held her breath each time she moved down a step. She gripped the banister tight; her knuckles white. At the bottom step she stopped, her eyes trying to adjust to the darkness. She sank down on the bottom step and pulled on her slippers.

Standing up again, she quickly grabbed the banister. Disorientated by the total darkness she began to wobble. *I'm going to fall!* Her arm shot out and one hand smacked onto the wall. She held her breath, listening for any sounds until she regained her balance. Keeping her hand on the wall and stretching out the other in front of her, she crept down the hallway until her fingertips felt the edge of the door frame. She took one small step further and placed her ear against the dining room door, the cold surface making her flinch. There was no sound. She felt for the door handle, then wrapped her fingers around it as if holding a flower. Pressing down on the handle, it moved as far as it would go and, after pausing for a moment, she pushed the door open a fraction. She waited again, listening hard, but all was still. With her nerves fluttering in her stomach, Emily slid her hand over the wall inside the room until she felt the light switch. The switch clicked and the lights in the room came on. The total quiet remained. Pushing the door further open, she peeked into the room and saw the instruments. Emily opened the door wider and put her head through the gap. She quickly looked behind it. There was nothing there. Her eyes swept round the room. She let go of the door handle until it returned without sound to its normal position. She stepped forward into the room, unconsciously leaving the door half open as an instinctive escape route. Emily walked slowly towards the drums, her eyes darting left and right, until she was about three feet away from them. Then she stopped and stared at the big brass cymbal. She shivered, glanced quickly behind her, and then returned her eyes to the cymbal. Clenching her fists, her eyes now focused only on the cymbal, she spoke.

"Did you really talk?" she said in barely a whisper. The room remained silent. Feeling braver, she continued in a low voice, "I'm sure I heard a voice; I'm sure I heard you talk." She waited.

"You did," came a melodious voice from behind her.

Emily whipped round, her breath caught in her throat, every muscle gripped with fear. With hard shallow breaths and churning stomach, her bulging eyes flickered all around the room in a frenzied dance. Cold hands squeezed her pounding heart and she could not move.

"Who said that?" she whispered.

"Me," came the reply.

"Who are you?" croaked Emily, her body still shivering and shaking.

"My name's Veronica," the voice replied. "I'm the violin down the table near the end. We heard you slap the wall just now and also heard you scream and talk a few hours ago. We were not sure if we heard what you said properly. Now we know." She paused and then continued. "Come closer to me so I can see you. Don't be afraid. No one will hurt you. We can all talk but we cannot move."

Emily edged her way down the table keeping slightly away from it until Veronica spoke again. "Keep coming, I'm the next violin you will see." Emily took another step and then she was looking into ravishing blue eyes and the luscious, smiling lips of Veronica.

"You are a special person," began Veronica. "What is your name?" she asked.

"Emily," the young girl replied.

"What a lovely name," Veronica replied. "I have had a

little time to adjust since you were last in this room, time to actually realise what has happened. I always knew that someday a person would hear us talk and understand what we were saying, but I never imagined it would happen to me. You are extraordinary, so rare that most instruments do not believe that you could ever exist. But here you are, talking to me, an old violin who thought she had been discarded forever, here together with my friends. We had all thought our useful lives were over. You are the living proof that what I always thought was true is actually true." She stopped talking and looked into Emily's wide, incredulous eyes.

"The lady you heard talking was Camilla, Camilla Caley. She's the big brass cymbal, part of Dean's drum kit," Veronica continued.

"Camilla, Dean," said Emily, confused. "You all have names?"

"Yes, we all have names just like you do," Veronica replied.

The other instruments were silent. They were still in utter, dumbfounded shock. Amazed and astounded, their belief that no person could ever hear them lay shattered, and they listened in awe to this young girl speaking with Veronica. This huge impact was lost on Emily. She had no understanding of the massive difference she had made to their lives.

"Well," continued Veronica, "I will introduce you to my friends."

Emily's mind was in a whirlwind. She heard the Hi's and Hello's, noticed eyes of hazel, blue, violet, and brown belonging to violins, Vera, Violet, Verity and Vivianne, but much did not register in her brain. It was overwhelming. She heard the funny voice of Charles the clarinet who drawled, "Delighted to make your acquaintance," and Celia the cello who, in her soft breathy voice, said, "Extremely nice to meet you." Theodore trumpet, Teddy trombone and Danny double bass all greeted her with twinkling eyes and smiling lips.

"We older instruments have only just met Dean and Camilla," continued Veronica, "but may I introduce Garry the lead guitar."

"Hi, sweet thing," he said.

"Gilbert, the base guitar."

"Dig meeting ya, babe."

"Then there's Caddie and Coral, they are the twin little cymbals."

"Hello Emily," they giggled.

"And the lady you first heard talking is their mother, Camilla, the big cymbal," Veronica continued.

"Delighted to meet you, Emily," said Camilla. "Thanks again for giving my sinuses a good blow through."

"Lastly, but not at all least, there's Dean the drum kit," said Veronica finally.

Dean grunted a short "Hello," and, after a pause, continued, "and I ain't stupid either."

"Oh, I'm so sorry, Dean," cried Emily, her voice full of genuine apology. "I didn't mean to be nasty to you. I think I was just a bit mad at the time." Emily struggled to find more and better words to show how sorry she was but Dean started talking again.

"OK," he said, "apology accepted, but just because I get thumped around a lot with sticks don't mean I ain't got no feelings. Let's start over again. Very pleased to meet you, Emily," he said.

"Happy to meet you too, Dean," Emily replied.

There was a short silence, which was broken by Charles clarinet. "It would seem, dear colleagues, that we have been blessed," he drawled in his cultured voice.

Emily went to the dining room door and closed it. All her fear had disappeared. This was excitement like she had never dreamed of.

"Is it only you who can hear us," asked Verity the violin, "or can the others hear us, too?"

"My friends think they can hear you," replied Emily, "but some are not totally sure. I don't think the grown-ups can."

"That makes it a lot easier, I suppose," replied Veronica. "Grown-ups would probably go and do something stupid if they knew they had instruments that could talk. Listen everybody, and this includes you Emily," she continued, "we must try to keep this wonderful miracle a secret. We must not talk to each other when any grown- up or strangers are near or in the same room. If they see us all talking together, that could lead to us being taken away from the children."

"Can you hear everything," asked Emily, "even the grown-ups? How long have you been here and how did you get here and what did you do before?" The questions tumbled out of Emily, one after another.

"Slow down, Emily," chuckled Danny the double bass in a deep soothing voice. "One thing at a time. It will take a while to answer all that. To answer your first question, yes, we can hear everything, including the grown-ups."

They began to tell her all about themselves, and it took quite a while.

When they had finished, Veronica asked Emily, "Anyway, what about you children; how did you get here? You don't look like brothers and sisters, you're too different."

Emily launched into a brief history of each of her friends as best she knew it, which, for some of them, was a bit sketchy.

"And what about you Emily?" asked Verity. "You have not told us about yourself."

Emily hesitated. She did not want to open the door to her memories again. Finally, she spoke and told them that she did not remember too much of when she was really little. Biting her lip and fighting back the tears that threatened to erupt, she whispered, "My mummy and daddy are dead, 'bout three years ago, car accident."

A collective sigh of deep pity flowed out from all of the instruments.

"Oh, you poor child," said Camilla, "you poor, poor child." Seconds of silence passed; the room was still, each with their own thoughts.

"OK," Emily said, returning to the subject of the grown-ups. "I will tell everyone to keep quiet when any grown-ups are around." She was just about to say something more when a sudden noise made her jump. Her head flicked around and she saw the door of the dining room open.

"Why Emily child," said Mrs Hutchins, who had seen the chink of light coming from underneath the dining room door on her way to her kitchen and had opened the door to investigate. "What are you doing here all on your own at this time in the morning? Are you all right?"

While Mrs Hutchins was talking, Emily managed to collect her thoughts. She smiled and said cheerfully, "Hi, Mrs Hutchins. I could not sleep much, so I got up early and came down to look at the instruments again."

"Oh," replied Mrs Hutchins, "so long as you're OK, that's fine then. I'm going to start getting the breakfast ready now. Do you want to help me?"

"I'll be there in a minute, Mrs Hutchins," she replied.

"Good girl," replied Mrs Hutchins, who left to go to her kitchen, closing the dining room door behind her.

"I have to go now, everyone," Emily whispered, as she did not want Mrs Hutchins to hear her through the kitchen hatch. "I'll be back later." And she went to join Mrs Hutchins in the kitchen. Miss Marigold joined them a few minutes later for her usual cup of tea and chat with Mrs Hutchins.

"Good morning, Mrs Hutchins," she said, and then after a short pause, "Oh, hello Emily. I didn't see you there at first. You're up early."

"Yes, Miss," Emily replied. "Like I said to Mrs Hutchins, I couldn't sleep, so I got up early to look at the instruments again."

"Oh, I see," answered Miss Marigold. "Are you feeling better this morning?"

Emily nodded.

"Be a good girl, Emily, and fetch those cups back from the TV room that you took with you yesterday evening," said Mrs Hutchins.

"OK, Mrs Hutchins," said Emily cheerfully, and she skipped out of the kitchen whistling her little tune.

"She seems to be her old self again," said Miss Marigold to Mrs Hutchins. "I got a bit worried about her yesterday evening."

"Kids are resilient," replied Mrs Hutchins. "They soon get over things. I'll be glad if Miss Stratton can get a record or something so that Emily can learn more of that little tune of hers. Now that would be nice." She ended with a chuckle.

"It sure would," replied Miss Marigold, and they both laughed.

Emily could hardly contain herself. She longed for breakfast to be over so that she could tell the others about the instruments. Finally, the time came, and as they had about ten minutes before class started, Emily whispered that she had something to tell them in the TV room. When all the children were there, Emily gave a quick explanation of what had occurred. She also passed on the message from

Veronica that they should not try talking to the instruments if there were any grown-ups or strangers around.

"Is that all really true, Emily?" asked Grace, her eyes and mouth wide open. "I mean really, really, really true? I know we said yesterday that we all thought we heard that voice, but now I'm not so sure."

Emily nodded. "If you don't believe me, try talking to them yourself."

Chapter 10

"Good morning again everyone," said Miss Stratton, smiling as she walked into the dining room. "As I said yesterday, today we will clean the instruments so that we can take a good look at them."

Emily went up to Miss Stratton and, in a low voice, said, "I'm sorry about yesterday, Miss," she began, "I would really like to do the drums now if that's still OK?"

Miss Stratton was touched. "Of course you may, Emily, and thank you for your apology; that was very sweet of you," Miss Stratton replied. "OK children, do you all remember what you have to do?" asked Miss Stratton. They all nodded and Mrs Hutchins flicked out her long tape measure.

"Let's get to it then," said Miss Stratton, "but be careful and gentle. Just take off as much dust as you can, don't rub too hard, and if you're not sure about anything, come and get me," she concluded. The dusters and cleaning brushes came out of the bags and the children got themselves sorted out. Touching the instruments as if they were made of very thin glass, the children slowly began the cleaning. For the first hour, Miss Stratton fussed around checking that everything was going well. She then announced that she and Miss Marigold were going to their offices and should they need further help, then Brandon could come and get them. Mrs Hutchins had gone to the classroom in order to start making the patterns on Miss Stratton's large desk table. The children were alone with the instruments.

"Hi Dean, hi Camilla, hi twins," said Emily as soon as Miss Stratton and Miss Marigold had left the room.

"Why, hello again dear child," said Camilla.

"Hi Emily," giggled Caddie and Coral.

"Hi, little sugar," said Dean with real warmth in his

90

voice. "Real glad you came to us 'cause we all think you're special," continued Dean. "In a way that makes us even happier, 'cause out of all the instruments in this room, we're special too. We are the only percussion folks here."

"What's percussion mean, Dean?" asked Emily.

"Well," replied Dean, "we got what is known as 'resonating surfaces'. That means we vibrate. We make our sounds when we get hit with a stick, or with your hand, or something like that. All the other instruments you either got to blow into, or do something with their strings. The other instruments can also make different notes, but each of us only has one note. That's why we are a drum kit, different sizes of drums to make different notes. It's the same with Camilla and the twins."

"The great thing for us," said Camilla, "is that we can listen to the rest of the band without having to worry about making the right sounds. Someone gives us a bash and we just sing right out. It's like having the best seats in the house."

"And the other big thing," said Dean, "is that we're in charge. We make the beat. Everyone else has to follow us. We can also play around when we want to with different drum rolls and stuff. We're pretty much free agents. So really, we've got it all."

Brandon was thinking hard as he began to clean the neck of the lead guitar. He did not want to make a fool of himself, and yet he could not contain his curiosity. Turning slightly away from the room so that he was looking into a corner, he said in a soft voice out of the corner of his mouth, "Can you hear me?" He nearly dropped the guitar when two grey eyes popped open on the headstock. "Sure man," came the reply, "but why are you talkin' so funny?" asked Gary.

"I wasn't sure if what Emily told us was all for real, even though I thought I heard a voice last night," answered Brandon in a whisper.

91

"Oh yeah," said Gary. "That was Camilla, super lady, but a memory like a sieve. Veronica was real mad with her but hey, we all make mistakes, and apart from that, she's got class. Me, Gilbert, Dean and the twins, we all love her to bits. Which one of the boys are you? I can't remember all the names Emily told us."

"Brandon," he replied.

"Pleased to meet ya again, Brandon," said Gary. "Say, take it a bit easy when you get further down. That's where my pickups are and they're real sensitive."

"OK," said Brandon, "I'll be careful."

Max had been listening to this conversation and was plucking up the courage to begin talking to the bass guitar he was cleaning but, just before he was about to open his mouth, two brown eyes suddenly opened on the headstock.

"Pardon me for, a-breakin' in on ya thoughts man, but I'm feelin' kinda lonely and left out here," murmured Gilbert in a dreamy tone.

Max was momentarily startled but then blurted out, "Sorry, I didn't intend to ignore you."

"It's no sweat man," replied Gilbert, "but nice to meet ya all the same. My name's Gilbert, by the way."

"Mine's Max," answered Max. "How are you?"

"Cool man, cool," replied Gilbert. "Just stayin' a bit loose an' easy for the mo. Nice movement with the duster, by the way," continued Gilbert, and he then began talking about wrist and finger movements. Soon Max found himself listening to the meaning of life, well, the meaning of life according to Gilbert, and asking all sorts of questions.

The children became so absorbed in their conversations with the instruments that by the time they realised that Miss Stratton and Miss Marigold had come back into the room it was too late.

"What are you all up to?" said Miss Stratton with a slightly raised eyebrow and enquiring smile. There was a moment's silence.

"It's a game, Miss," said Emily.

"Oh yes," said Miss Stratton. "What sort of game?"

"Well, you know I thought I had heard the cymbal thing talk yesterday," said Emily, "well, we talked about it last night and thought it would be fun if the instruments really could talk and we could talk back to them. So, we said we would make it a game and treat them like friends, like a doll or a cat."

"I see," said Miss Stratton, her eyebrows still arched. "And what about you Brandon, are you playing the game, too?"

Thinking with the speed of light to find an answer that would not make him look stupid or seem less responsible in Miss Stratton's eyes, he replied, "Yes, Miss. I didn't want to be a spoilsport so I joined in so not to ruin it for the others."

Miss Stratton was silent for a moment and then she laughed and said, "OK. If you're having fun, you just keep right on doing it. Anyway," she continued, "it's now time for lunch."

As they left the dining room, Brandon sidled up to Emily and said, "Emily, you are a genius."

She looked up at Brandon and smiled with a face full of surprise and delight. Brandon put his arm around her shoulder and pulled her to him, and together they walked into the kitchen. A warm glow spread through her, filling her with a billowing cloud of contentment. She felt warm, wanted and cared for, and another piece that had been missing from her for so long, returned in a burst of dazzling joy.

"Did you all talk to the instrument you were cleaning?" asked Emily in a hushed, excited voice when the children were all gathered later that day in the TV room.

"Yeah, we did," said Brandon and Max. "We talked to the guitars," Brandon continued, "Emily was not telling fibs when she said they can talk. They really can. It's something weird, but it's true."

"Told you so," said Emily. "I told you they could talk."

"What did the guitars say?" asked Freya.

"Well, we didn't say much, just our names, and he told me to be careful with his pickups," answered Brandon. "Max talked a lot more."

"What did ya say Max? Tell us, tell us," said Rachael.

"The bass guitar, his name is Gilbert," said Max. "He's, well, a bit weird, no, really weird, but real interesting at the same time. Didn't understand a lot of it, all a bit deep for me, but he seems real nice."

Faith and Jasmine both told the others about Celia, how she was so overjoyed about what was happening. She had been feeling very low and sad but now was ecstatically happy.

They continued relaying their stories and there were frequent interruptions with, "Violet said the same," and "Danny had played at that place too."

All the instruments had made similar comments, that they thought they would never feel hands again, never again feel the kiss of sensitive fingertips on their strings or the warm air of life blowing through them. They had all thought their lives were over, left alone to fade away. But now, a miracle. The myth was actually true, and they were the luckiest and most special instruments in all the world. At the same time, they were humble that they had been chosen.

Miss Stratton, Miss Marigold and Mrs Hutchins had all gone upstairs to their sitting room and the children left the TV room and returned to the instruments in the dining room.

"Hello there," said Veronica, when she saw Emily looking over her. "Back again? I haven't had so much attention since

94

I was a young thing and got my first outing to a concert," she said.

Emily asked Veronica if she had heard what she had said to Miss Stratton about playing a game when she had heard them all talking.

"I heard you," said Veronica. "I suppose it was bound to happen at some point but as your grown-ups can't hear us, it does not really matter. We will still try not to talk when grown-ups are around, but at least now they shouldn't take any notice if they hear you talking to us. So, don't worry about it at all, Emily. Everything will be fine. Anyway," she continued, "would you mind standing us all up so we can see each other better? Lying on your back for so much time can get awfully sore."

Emily told the others what Veronica had requested, and so they arranged the instruments standing upright on the floor leaning against the chairs to form a small semi-circle.

"That's much better, thanks," said Veronica.

The instruments chatted with each other in a bit of light banter. Jokes and jibes about how they had aged, put on weight, the state of their strings, had your rollers on too hot again darling etc., and then Veronica spoke to the children, many of whom were staring at the instruments in amazement.

"We know from Emily that you can all hear us, and we can all hear you. I will make the introductions again so we all know who we are and then take it from there."

Veronica introduced all the instruments again and all the children did likewise to the instruments.

"Well," continued Veronica, "you may wonder why I have been doing most of the talking so far. I am the first chair violin, orchestrally speaking that is. If I was the first violin ever made, I would be in a museum somewhere. This means that I am the sort of leader for the orchestral instruments here. Dean, Camilla, Gary, Gilbert and the twins over there, they are from a different set-up altogether, and I will let them explain that themselves, as I do not know enough about them to do it. I only know what they have told me so far. Meeting them is a whole new experience for me too. I will just ask a couple of things and then pass you over to Gary and his band. First, have any of you played an instrument before?" All the children shook their heads.

"OK," continued Veronica, "so, I don't suppose any of you can read music either?" Again, the children's head moved from side to side.

"Well," said Veronica, "that makes things a bit harder, but not impossible. So long as you can all hear and can hold a tune in your heads, we should be able to teach you the basics at any rate. That go for you and your guys and ladies too, Gary?"

"Sure, Veronica, we can do the same," answered Gary.

"Fine," said Veronica. "Now, over to you then, Gary."

"We're a rock band," started off Gary. "You know our kind of music?" This question was answered by vigorous nods.

"Good," continued Gary, "then I don't have to explain too much. He told them what each group member did, finishing off with, "Dean makes the beat and we follow that." There was a brief silence.

"That you done, Gary?" asked Veronica.

"Yeah, thanks Veronica," Gary answered, "for the time bein' anyhow."

"OK," continued Veronica, "I don't know there's much else we can do at the moment except chat and have a laugh. Before we can move on," she continued, looking at the broken strings and the nasty bend and dent that Teddy the trombone had, "somehow we've got to get fixed.""

It was exactly the same question that was giving Miss Stratton her second sleepless night. She too had realised that one of the first things she needed to do was get the instruments repaired – somehow.

After making three telephone calls, one to the Music Shop in the city, and two more to other musical companies, asking about repairs to musical instruments, Miss Stratton was shocked by the prices they had quoted her, even just for inspecting the instruments, let alone repairing them. If she could not jump this hurdle, then the project could go no further, and she desperately sought inspiration in how to overcome the problem. Somewhat gloomy, with the threat of such an early defeat looming large over the horizon, Miss Stratton got up and quietly made herself a cup of tea. Sitting in her dressing gown, she explored every avenue she could think of, but still, she could not find a solution. She got up, still in her dressing gown, and went down to her office to try and work through the heap of paperwork on her desk. She began filling out various forms and reports. The next question on the form she was completing asked for the petty cash total; she unlocked the drawer in her desk and opened it.

The piece of paper triggered a surge of hope into Miss Stratton's mind. The piece of paper, with the name of that little tune Emily was always whistling and which Miss Stratton had put in the drawer for safekeeping, appeared as a lifeboat to a sinking ship. Picking up the paper, Miss Stratton looked at the printed side. Taking her telephone directory and, hoping against hope that she would find what she so desperately needed, she scanned the pages until, with a leap of her heart, she saw it.

Chapter 11

She half lay on her sofa, her arms folded and her eyes closed, the music from the record player taking her to a floating place of peace. Then another unconnected, jarring noise entered her consciousness, and it took her a few startled seconds to realise it was her telephone ringing. Quickly getting up, she pressed the pause button on the record player and picked up the phone.

"Hello," she said. "Elizabeth Rose speaking."

Somehow, some speck of reason had always, at the last second, made her pull back from stepping off the lethal edge of no return that six months ago had often been in front her. The destructive black moods of despair had been on the brink of claiming their ultimate victory more than once, but clinging on by one fragile, aching fingernail, with no logical explanation, she had resisted, and against the odds she had survived. With painful slowness, the periods in dark places became fewer. Step by little step, she was rebuilding her life.

"Good afternoon, Miss Rose. My name is Miss Stratton, and I believe we met a couple of days ago at the Music Shop in the new shopping complex in the city."

"Oh yes, I remember," replied Elizabeth warmly. "You were looking for dusters and cleaning brushes together with your young girls."

"That's right," said Miss Stratton, "and you were kind enough to write down the name of a piece of music for us on a piece of paper, the name of a tune one of my girls was whistling. On the back of that piece of paper was your name and address, through which I have been able to find your telephone number."

"That's right," laughed Elizabeth. "I remembered before I left the shop that those details were on the other side."

"Before I begin with the reason for my call," continued Miss Stratton, "I deeply apologise for the rather dark operation of finding your telephone number, and also to ask if I have caught you at a bad moment?"

"Not at all, Miss Stratton," replied Elizabeth. "How can I help you?"

Taking a deep breath, Miss Stratton explained that the three girls were not her own, in that she was not their natural mother, or perhaps more appropriately, their grandmother. They were three of the children in her care. Miss Stratton did not wish to play a sympathy card, or create any feeling of moral obligation onto Miss Rose, but there was no other way to say it.

"I am the principal of an orphanage, Miss Rose, and I have thirteen children at present in my care."

"I see," said Elizabeth, but she could not help saying it without a noticeable degree of sympathy and compassion.

"Well," continued Miss Stratton, "the children are busy with a project about which they are, for the moment anyway, very enthusiastic. But we've hit a bit of a problem. We have some musical instruments that are in need of some repair, but to be perfectly frank, Miss Rose, the prices I have been told so far are, well, simply beyond our means. I hope you will forgive my rudeness, but I thought that as you seemed to be very knowledgeable on the subject of music, which I freely admit I am not, you might know of a musical company that I could contact whose fees are a bit cheaper? I am sorry to have to trouble you this way, but to be honest, I have run out of routes to follow."

Elizabeth felt a chill pass through her when she heard the words "musical instruments". She had an uneasy feeling in the pit of her stomach. Suppressing the little shiver that had tensed her back, and ignoring the goose-bumps on her arms, Elizabeth focused her mind. As it had become second nature to her over the last four months since working at the city's housing department, she asked Miss Stratton for her telephone number. Miss Stratton gave Elizabeth this information, and she wrote it down on the notepad next to her telephone.

"So, Miss Rose, do you know of anybody who could possibly help us out?" Miss Stratton concluded.

Pausing for a moment, Elizabeth fought the worrying feeling that was building up inside her. "Maybe I do know someone who could help but it may take a while as he is usually very busy. I could get in touch with him and ask him what he could do. Where is your orphanage, Miss Stratton, so I can tell the person I am thinking of where you are?" Elizabeth asked, her voice strained and nervous. She was not in control. She was, without choice, on a train, going to a single, unknown destination. She did not know exactly where that place was, only that she did not want to go there.

Miss Stratton gave the name of the orphanage and the address.

Cold fingers of ice closed around Elizabeth's heart and they began to squeeze. Her stomach tensed and churned. Her legs became wet rolls of newspaper and she gripped the edge of the telephone table with her free hand, knuckles white and fingertips digging. "I'm sorry," croaked Elizabeth. "I'll call you back." She fumbled with the receiver as she tried to replace it, gripped the table with her other hand and crumpled to her knees.

The anger had faded, the bitterness less sharp, but the heartache of sadness remained as strong as ever. The guilt and admission to herself that if she had acted quicker, made the decisions that now in hindsight seemed so obvious, then the destruction of her dreams would maybe not have happened six months ago. Unable to move, her head bowed and resting on the table, she began to sink back into that black pool she had been trying so hard to escape from. Her forehead was hurting where it leant against the edge of her telephone table, so she tried to stand. The effort was partially successful and, with legs half bent, she stumbled across the room to her sofa and collapsed onto it. For many months she could not bear to listen to music, to think about music or to read about music. It hurt too much. Her previous passion had not turned to total hatred but was suppressed, no longer of interest, no longer part of who she was. It was only in the past three weeks that she had managed, shakily, to put on her record player. The sounds had somehow managed to reach the fragments of warm embers that were buried under the grey ashes. At first it was difficult, but gradually she rediscovered the comfort that beautiful music could give her.

Now she knew where the train was going and it filled her with fear. She wanted to get off, but at the same time she knew she wanted to help those children. The wide-eyed faces of the girls that she had seen in the shop were projected in front of her eyes. Rising from her sofa, she walked on unsteady legs back to her telephone, picked up the receiver and dialled the number she had written on the pad.

Miss Stratton was shocked and totally confused by the sudden ending of the telephone call. She wondered what could possibly have happened, and the problem she had with the instrument repairs now seemed twice as big and twice as heavy on her shoulders. She sat and waited, willing the telephone to ring, and finally it did. Picking up the receiver, she once again heard Elizabeths' voice but it was heavier and somehow sadder.

"I'm so sorry for breaking off so quickly just now," said

Elizabeth, "but I sort of swallowed the wrong way and I thought I was going to have a coughing fit. I'm OK again now."

"No problem at all my dear," Miss Stratton replied. "I've been in that situation myself sometimes." In reality, Miss Stratton found it difficult to believe what Elizabeth had just said. There was something else, but now was not the moment to ask questions.

"The person I am thinking of has a workshop on the outskirts of the city," Elizabeth said.

"Oh," replied Miss Stratton. "Would we have to take the instruments there?" She voiced the question in a tone that indicated that that may be difficult.

Elizabeth felt the train picking up speed. She knew that Mario Rozetti, her friend and instrument repairer, did not normally like leaving his workshop, so continuing after a brief hesitation she found herself saying, "It would maybe save a lot of time if I could come and see the instruments first. Depending on their condition, I could perhaps get an idea from the repairer of what it would cost to repair them and let you know."

Miss Stratton felt a great surge of gratitude towards Miss Rose and replied.

"Are you really sure you want to go to that much trouble on our behalf, Miss Rose? I hope you do not feel obliged to do this for any reasons created by our situation here," she concluded.

"It's OK, Miss Stratton," Elizabeth replied. "If we could fix a convenient day and time I will come and take a look." The day and time were agreed.

Replacing her receiver, Elizabeth returned to her sofa. She sat down and then let her head fall into her hands. What had she just done? Why had she not tried to get off the train? Why had she agreed to go to the orphanage and look at the instruments? She was exposed, vulnerable, and the snakes writhed and slithered inside her waiting to strike.

The newly repainted name board was still there, in the same place, the same colour, the same size, and although the lettering style was unchanged, the words on the sign had been altered. The bottom of the board was now blank with no words on it at all. The sign now simply read, "Saint Etheldreda's Foundation". Standing on the wide pavement on the other side of the road, Elizabeth stared at the board. The journey from her home to the spot where she now stood had been difficult, nerve-racking and wretched, but she was now at her destination.

Her eyes moved over the façade of the building. The white paint of the window frames had not been touched, but it had not deteriorated much since she had last looked at them so many months before. The windows had all been very nicely cleaned though, and they sparkled in the morning sunlight. Summoning up every ounce of willpower, she checked for traffic and quickly crossed the road. The steps to her gallows were before her, and she knew she had to climb them. With each step, another heavy sack of sadness was added to her already burdened shoulders, but she managed to reach the top. Three more paces brought her to the familiar door. Half raising her hand with a single finger outstretched, she paused, and then, before she could change her mind, her finger was on the button, pressing it hard.

She heard the bell ringing inside and, after half a minute or so, she heard the muffled footsteps and a key scuffing in a lock. The door opened.

Tall. Erect. Commanding. The grey-haired lady whom Elizabeth had met two days previously at the Music Shop stood in the open doorway. Miss Stratton's smile was wide and warm. She stretched out her hand in greeting and said,

"How lovely to meet you again Miss Rose. Please, do come in."

Elizabeth, who was using every scrap of energy to maintain the fixed smile on her face, took Miss Stratton's warm, firm hand and shook it.

"It's nice to meet you again, Miss Stratton," Elizabeth replied with a slightly unsteady voice as she stepped inside the hall.

Almost immediately, Miss Stratton noticed something odd. Most people, when coming somewhere new, allowed their eyes to wander in order to take in more of their surroundings. Miss Rose, she noticed, did not do this, but kept her eyes fixed on one point. First it was the wall of the hallway and then, as they walked to Miss Stratton's office, Miss Rose kept her eyes fixed on the floor ahead looking neither up, nor down, left nor right. Miss Stratton was puzzled. After arriving at her office and asking Miss Rose to be seated, Miss Stratton asked her visitor if she would like some tea.

"No, thank you," answered Elizabeth.

Miss Stratton saw that she was still looking straight ahead. She had the strange feeling that Miss Rose must have been here before, that she knew the rooms of this building and it made her uncomfortable. The strange and abrupt ending of her first telephone call added to Miss Stratton's unease.

"I do not wish to be rude, Miss Rose," said Miss Stratton with a soft voice, "but have I done or said something that has upset you?"

Elizabeth looked down at the floor. She was fighting and losing her internal battle. With a deep sigh, she placed her hands on Miss Stratton's desk as if to steady herself and then looked up. "This used to be Saint Etheldreda's Music School," said Elizabeth. The moment the words were out of her mouth, she felt the dampness form around the bottom of her eyes.

"Yes, that's right," replied Miss Stratton.

"It was my school," said Elizabeth. "I had to close it because not enough people came here after the new music school opened in the city." There was a short silence.

"That must have been very painful for you, my dear," replied Miss Stratton, with sincere compassion. "I can imagine it still hurts, which makes me even more grateful that you have come." In an automatic movement of a caring mother, Miss Stratton reached out and placed her hand on top of Miss Rose's hand and very gently squeezed it. Elizabeth could not contain the quick, choked sob that instantly burst from her throat. She began to rise from the chair. "I'm sorry," she said. "I'm being stupid. I should go now and do this at another time."

Miss Stratton was having none of it. Still squeezing Elizabeth's hand, she took it in both of hers; moved around her desk; knelt in front of Elizabeth and looked up into her face.

"Do not let the darkness win," she said. "It is easy to give in. I know, I have been in a very dark place like you are now, but you must fight it. The brighter times are out there waiting for you if only you would reach out to them. Let your sadness out, let the dark clouds go. Talk to me and I will try to help you get there."

Elizabeth began to mumble, stumbling over her words. She looked into Miss Stratton's caring eyes and found herself talking as she had never done before; a doorway had opened in her mind and outside of the door there was sunshine. The chains had loosened, the hangman's noose taken from around her neck. She opened the sluice gates to her heart and let the stored, stagnant, poisonous waters of her pain flood out, their force taking all the debris of her misery with them. And then she was still.

105

"We must all move on, Miss Rose," said Miss Stratton with tender understanding. "Maybe this was your moment to do so. Come to my rooms and freshen up," continued Miss Stratton. "You will feel much better then."

An artist can use the same piece of canvas more than once. The original picture can be painted over with a layer of white, creating a new, blank surface on which to make a new composition. The first picture is still there, but it is hidden, unseen, and it can no longer create emotions. Only if the new painting is damaged, or the new paint is peeled back, can it again be seen and its power to evoke feelings return. Having let go of her inner, dark turmoil, the picture of Elizabeth's past had been covered with a layer of bright white. A new palette of colours had been mixed, and the brush was in the artist's hand, ready to begin. Elizabeth did not know if the brush strokes would be bold and raw, or if they would be gentle and flowing. But she had a new optimism that the colours would be lighter and brighter, even though at that moment she had no idea what the picture would look like when it was finished.

Relaxed, and sitting in Miss Stratton's sitting room with a hot, strong cup of coffee, Miss Stratton asked Elizabeth if she would like to see the instruments and their storage boxes.

"I would love to," Elizabeth replied and, after finishing her coffee, she accompanied Miss Stratton to the second floor where they looked at the instruments leaning against the walls and those in the blue storage boxes.

"These are very good boxes for the instruments," said Elizabeth. "Where did you get them?"

"There is quite a story attached to that, Miss Rose, and if you don't mind, I would rather tell you when we have a nice long time to enjoy it," replied Miss Stratton, with a rather mischievous smile on her face.

"I'll look forward to that," replied Elizabeth, laughing.

Elizabeth took her time and looked at all the instruments. They were all old friends to her, but she felt no pangs of loss. Quite the opposite: she was thrilled with the thought that they were going to be used again. She made some notes, but basically it wasn't too bad. Some violins had broken strings, but there was nothing special about that. The worst damage seemed to be to the trombone, and the keys on the clarinet needed some serious attention as well.

It was a good two hours later when Elizabeth finally left Saint Etheldreda's Foundation. She promised Miss Stratton that she would visit her friend, the instrument repairer, as soon as she could and report back to her. Taking the bus back into the city, Elizabeth checked her watch and noted that, in fact, she had plenty of time to go and see Mario that afternoon. With no other pressing things that needed her time or attention, she changed buses at the city bus station and took a ticket to the nearest bus stop to where Mario had his workshop. Walking from the bus stop, she entered a plain street that had various small shops along each side, until she came to Mario's shop. Entering the premises, Elizabeth knew the routine. When Mario was working, he gave the task in hand his utmost concentration. The button on the counter in the shop was connected to a light in the workshop. When Mario or one of his sons saw the light, they would enter the shop to see who was there. If they were all busy with delicate operations, then the person in the shop would just have to wait until somebody was ready.

Mario Rozetti had earned himself an excellent reputation as one of the most highly skilled repairers of musical instruments in the country. Musicians travelled a very long way for his services. He had built this reputation over a long period and had more than enough business, not only to keep himself well occupied but also three of his children, whom he had taught and brought into the business.

Elizabeth rang the bell once and waited. After about five minutes, a youngish man, of Mediterranean descent, opened the door. A big smile lit up his face as he recognised Elizabeth. They gave each other a hug. Alfredo was one of Mario's sons and, after the usual kissing on both cheeks, Elizabeth enquired if his father was in.

"Yeah, he's here," replied Alfredo. "Come through; he's in the workshop."

Elizabeth followed Alfredo into a bright workshop with dozens of different tools gleaming from the walls around the work benches. Elizabeth saw Mario deep in concentration, working with what looked like parts of a trumpet. Elizabeth and Alfredo stood still, watching and waiting until Mario looked up.

"Someone to see you, Pa," said Alfredo, smiling. Mario, on seeing Elizabeth standing next to his son, came rushing forward, his mouth wide open in a huge smile, his arms outstretched.

"Elizabeth," he cried in a very thick Italian accent that he had never lost. Giving her a great hug and both kissing each other on both cheeks, he took her by the hand and told her that she should sit on one of the workbench stools. "How are you?" he cried. "Long time, long time, how you bin, you OK, yes?" The questions tumbled out one after the other with no pause for breath.

"Hi Mario," she replied, smiling. "I'm fine, I'm fine, and how are you?"

"Good, good," he replied.

"And your family?" continued Elizabeth.

"Ah," said Mario, throwing up his hands, "wife, children, grandchildren, can you do this, can you do that, can you do this?" He stopped and burst out laughing. "They are all good, yes, ver' good," replied Mario, his face a picture of contented happiness.

"Do you have a lot of work on at the moment, Mario?" Elizabeth asked.

"We always have plenty work," he replied, "but for friends and family, well, we can always arrange something."

Mario had a large family. His wife, Maria, whom he adored, seven children, four boys and three girls, all of whom were now married, and numerous grandchildren. He had told Elizabeth that he'd lost count of how many grandchildren he had, when she had last asked many months ago, but she had not believed him. With his children and grandchildren, he was as soft as cotton wool.

"So, Elizabeth, this a friendly visit or can I help you with my talents?" he asked.

"Both," answered Elizabeth, and told him about Saint Etheldreda's Foundation and what they were trying to do.

"Ver' sad when your school closed, ver' sad," he said with genuine feeling. "You OK now after that?" he asked.

"I am very well Mario," she replied, suddenly realising how much she had changed in just a few hours. "Yes," she continued, "I am feeling good," she said in a strong, confident tone.

"So," continued Mario, "what would you like me to do for you, Elizabeth?"

"I have made a list of the things that I could see when I inspected the instruments this morning Mario," Elizabeth replied, "but these are only the obvious things. If I could get the instruments to you, could you take a proper look and then give me some idea about what the cost would be to repair them?" Mario knew that Elizabeth had always taken very good care of her instruments, so he enquired how the damage had happened.

"Removals men," replied Elizabeth. "They were in a great hurry and not very careful."

Mario grunted, and then after a few moments asked, "If possible, if possible, it would be easier for me to inspect the instruments where they are now. As you can see, there is not so much space in here and besides, it would be nice to…" He let the sentence hang.

"The children?" interrupted Elizabeth.

Mario nodded. "I would like to meet them," he said simply.

"OK," said Elizabeth. "I will check with Miss Stratton, the principal, and let you know for sure. I don't see any problem, but it is better to check. How can I get in touch without coming over here?"

"Give me a call at home," he replied, and he gave her the best time to call.

"If everything is OK, Mario," Elizabeth said, "when do you think you can come?"

"I think Saturday afternoon around one o'clock would be best for me," replied Mario. "Is that OK for you? Will you be there?"

"That's fine with me, Mario and yes, I hope to be there if it's OK with the Foundation. Thanks Mario," she said. "I have to go now so that I have time to call the Foundation, but I will hopefully see you on Saturday at Saint Etheldreda's."

"Bye now Elizabeth, and you take care," replied Mario. "You can tell them that there will be no charge for the inspection," and he turned back to the parts on his workbench.

Elizabeth was back in her apartment. She went straight away to her telephone and called Saint Etheldreda's. Miss Marigold answered and, after saying hello, Elizabeth asked if Miss Stratton was available.

110

"Just a moment please, Miss Rose," replied Miss Marigold.

When Miss Stratton came on the phone, Elizabeth explained that she had been to see the instrument repairer and he had said he would prefer to look at the instruments at Saint Etheldreda's, rather than at his workshop. If this was OK for Miss Stratton, would Saturday afternoon at one o'clock be a good time for him to come? Lastly, she added, "There will be no charge for the inspection, Miss Stratton."

"I cannot thank you enough, Miss Rose," replied Miss Stratton, delighted with the news. "That has taken a big worry away."

"One thing, Miss Stratton," asked Elizabeth, "would it be OK if I came along as well?"

"My dear Miss Rose," replied Miss Stratton, "nothing could give me more pleasure."

After the call had ended, Miss Stratton returned to studying the post that had arrived that day. Miss Marigold first sorted out the letters, took out the important ones, and put them on Miss Stratton's desk. Today she had also left one letter that she had not opened. The sender's details were on the front of the envelope at the top. With a knot in her stomach, Miss Stratton opened the letter that the envelope told her was from the Juvenile Justice Court. She read slowly to make sure she understood everything in the letter correctly. The letter was short. It requested her presence at the Juvenile Justice Court and told her that Mr Robson from the Juvenile Support Department was also requested to attend. The date and time of the hearing completed the information contained in the letter. With so many things happening in such a short space of time, Miss Stratton had completely forgotten about the ongoing court hearing into the fire at the children's previous home. It created another worry in Miss Stratton's already overflowing mind, but as there was not much she could do at that moment, she did the only thing she could. She prayed that all that had been so far achieved at Saint Etheldreda's Foundation would not be damaged or destroyed, that all her hopes would not be ruined.

At her work, Elizabeth sat opposite a quiet, unmarried man around three years older than herself whose name was Stephen Hanney. He had helped her a lot when she had first started working at the housing department, and they had developed a casual friendship. He called her Lizzie, which at first, she did not like, but now had grown quite used to. Stephen drove a small van and he had offered it to her should she ever need to move any large objects around. She had once taken him up on his offer when she had bought a table for her apartment. He had given her his home address and telephone number and she had done the same. She waited until early evening and then dialled his number.

"Hello, Steve," she said when he picked up.

"Hello, Lizzie," he replied.

"Have you got anything planned for this Saturday afternoon?" she asked. "I need to get my record player to a place where I'm doing a bit of voluntary work," she continued, "and it would be difficult to do this on the bus."

"Should be OK," he said. "Don't think I have got anything on. Where do you need to go?"

Elizabeth gave him the name and address of the place she wanted to go to and they agreed he would come and collect her and the record player early on Saturday afternoon.

The day came and Stephen arrived at Elizabeth's apartment. They chatted for a few minutes and then Stephen loaded the record player into his van. Elizabeth got into the passenger seat beside him carrying a medium-sized shopping bag, which she kept on her lap. Arriving in the area near the Foundation, Stephen found a parking space and together they walked the short distance to Saint Etheldreda's. Elizabeth pressed the doorbell. The old door opened and they were greeted by Miss Marigold. After greeting each other with warm, inviting smiles, Elizabeth asked if there was somewhere she could put the record player, and Miss Marigold said it would be safe on the floor in a corner of her office. Once this had been done, Elizabeth thanked Stephen for all his help before he set off back to his van and went home. They parted with, "See you at the office next week."

Elizabeth returned to Miss Marigold's office and asked if Miss Stratton was around. "She's just upstairs at the moment, Miss Rose," replied Miss Marigold, "we had some furniture delivered late yesterday afternoon. She is busy getting that sorted out and the instruments ready for the inspection. She should be down any minute now." They chatted for a few minutes before Miss Stratton appeared.

"Hello, Miss Rose," said Miss Stratton, who was just about to ask about the inspection of the instruments when the front doorbell rang.

"I'll go," said Miss Marigold, and she hurried off to open the door. What greeted her was the biggest bunch of flowers she had ever seen. The flowers moved to one side, showing a stocky man with black curly hair, and a dazzling smile. Behind him stood another man in his early thirties with the same hair and complexion.

"Good afternoon," said Mario with his thick Italian accent. "My name is Mario Rozetti, and this is my son, Alfredo. I believe you are expecting us to look at some of your musical instruments."

Miss Marigold, whose mouth had been doing a pretty good imitation of a goldfish, was rescued when Elizabeth and Miss Stratton appeared.

"Mario, Alfredo!" cried Elizabeth, "what have you got there?"

"Pretty difficult to miss I'd say," said Miss Stratton with a laugh. She moved forward stretched out her hand and shook Mario's and Alfredo's hands with a welcoming smile.

"Welcome to Saint Etheldreda's," she said. "Please do come in, both of you."

Mario bowed and handed Miss Stratton the huge bunch of flowers and said, "Enchanted Madame. A small token for all the ladies here," he continued. "Your work is special, so you must be too."

Miss Stratton and Miss Marigold were temporarily speechless, but Elizabeth had simply mouthed a big "thank you" to Mario, who still stood outside the door beaming with pleasure.

"Oh, do come in the pair of you," exclaimed Miss Stratton after finding her voice again. "Thank you for such beautiful flowers, you really shouldn't have." Mario bowed again and gave Miss Stratton another dazzling smile.

"Small thing, small thing," he said.

"I will put these into a vase straightaway," said Miss Stratton. "So if you would be so kind as to go with these two ladies, I will be with you in a moment."

Alfredo picked up the two toolboxes they had brought with them and stepped inside the hall. Mario grinned at Elizabeth, who grinned back and whispered, "Charmer."

Declining the refreshment that Miss Stratton had offered on her return, Mario asked politely if they could now look at the instruments as they had to leave by half-past three at the latest to go and visit one of his daughters. Miss Stratton led Mario, Alfredo and Elizabeth up the stairs to the second floor and into the room where the instruments had been laid out on three white wooden tables. On the way up to the second floor, Mario had asked if the children were there and, after being told that they had been asked to stay in the TV room, Mario had suggested that it might be nice to see them, and if they were quiet, they could watch him at his work.

"Are you sure you don't mind, Mr Rozetti?" asked Miss Stratton. "But it would be nice if the children could see what you are going to do."

"Yes," replied Mario, "I like them to watch; that way they learn."

As soon as Mario, Alfredo and Elizabeth were in the room with the instruments, Miss Stratton went quickly downstairs to get the children.

The pounding stairs and excited babble of voices announced the children's arrival and soon they were all standing in the room. Miss Stratton introduced them to Elizabeth, Mario Rozetti and Alfredo. Elizabeth recognised the three girls she had met in the Music Shop and said, "Hello again," to them.

"Well then, my young friends," began Mario with a big smile. "I am very 'appy to meet you all and if you want to laugh at my funny accent, then please go right ahead. I laugh at it too," he concluded, his smiling face suddenly creasing up as he roared with laughter. Some of the children giggled.

Mario continued. "OK, my friends. I am now going to look at your instruments, so I want you to be very quiet." He turned to his work; serious concentration etched on his face. He picked up each of the smaller instruments and studied them closely, turning them around in his skilled hands. He tapped various parts of them gently with his fingertips and, after completing this, he moved on to the next instrument. The larger instruments took longer and he laid them on the floor so that he could inspect them closely.

After about twenty minutes, he walked back to where Miss Stratton, Elizabeth and the children were standing.

"No bad, no bad," he said. "A few broken strings which are no problem, they can easy be fixed. Only two very sick," he said, pointing at the trombone and the clarinet. "These I must take to my workshop. And now my young friends," he continued, "come here and stand in a semi-circle so you can all see." He quickly took one of the chairs that were stacked up near the wall and put it close to a table where some of the violins were lying. He arranged the children so they could all see, and then he began to explain to them in simple language the names of the different parts of the instrument and how to hold it properly. He then picked up a bow and explained the same. The children and Miss Stratton were mesmerised and hung on to his every word.

Looking at his watch to check how much time he had, Mario opened his toolbox and, after briefly glancing at the violin before him, he took out a small packet. Opening the packet, he pulled out a very thin coil of wire. "This is an 'E' string," he said, showing it to the children, "and now I am going to take out the broken one and put this new one in its place."

With years of skill and experience, Mario replaced the broken string, but he did it slowly so that the children could see exactly what he was doing.

"There," he said, "this instrument now only needs tuning and then it will be ready for playing."

He got up and moved to the next instrument on the table; the children following him. It did not take too long before all the instruments with broken strings had been repaired. He then took a beautiful, small, polished wooden box from his toolbox and opened it. Inside was a set of tuning forks; he took one out of the box and put it on the

116

table. He then picked up a piece of folded cloth from the toolbox and, after unwrapping it, he showed the children the block of amber resin.

"This is rosin," he said. "We need to rub this on the bow so that the hairs can grip the strings and make a sound. If we don't do this, then the bow will not make a note as it will just slide over the strings."

Mario picked up the bow that he had put down on the table and rubbed the block of rosin up and down the hairs five or six times. Pinching the arms of the tuning fork between his fingers, he quickly stood it on its base on the table, and a beautiful clear note sounded throughout the room. He then picked up the violin, placed the chin rest under his chin and drew the bow over the "A" string. The sound was terrible. He adjusted the "A" string peg slightly so that the note it produced was exactly the same as the note from the tuning fork. Using the "A" string as a reference, Mario drew the bow over the other strings, ending with the "E" string. He adjusted a small screw at the bottom end of the "E" string, which he told the children was called a "Fine Tuner", until he was happy with the note it made.

"There," he said, and, turning to Freya, who was standing closest to him. He handed her the violin and said, "Now you try." He helped Freya hold the violin and bow correctly and guided her hand as Freya drew the bow over the "E" string and played a clear note.

"Ver' good, ver' good," beamed Mario, taking back the instrument and putting it back on the table. "This instrument is now ready," he said. "OK," he continued, "Alfredo and I will rush a bit now and try to tune all the instruments for you before we go, and we have to go soon or…" He made a motion with his finger across his throat and everyone laughed.

The children were entranced, their eyes darting between

Mario and Alfredo as they began the tuning work. With tuning forks humming, strings were inspected for condition and tightened, the tuning slide on the trumpet was adjusted, the drums were tapped to see that their sounds were all compatible and two tiny adjustments were made to their tension rods.

Briefly talking to each other, Mario and Alfredo nodded and they returned their tools to their boxes.

"If it is OK for you, Madame, we will take the trombone and the clarinet back to our workshop for repair," said Mario. Miss Stratton nodded, but he had seen the little look of worry that had flashed across her face and he knew why it had happened.

They went back down to the hallway and, as Miss Stratton was about to open the door, Mario spoke in a soft voice. "Madame," he said, "not only do I admire and respect you for the work you do here, but there is also something else. For Italians at least," he continued, "family is ver' ver' important. So," he said finally, "do not think of money. There will be no cost to you for what I do for you, not now, not ever. Some things are far more importan' than money."

Miss Stratton, who for once felt hot tears rushing up to her eyes, kissed Mr Rozetti long and hard on both cheeks and shook Alfredo's hand with both of hers. She opened the door and managed to whisper the words, "thank you," without her tears spilling down her cheeks.

After Mario had given Miss Stratton another dazzling smile, he and Alfredo left. Regaining her composure, Miss Stratton asked Elizabeth how much longer she could stay.

"For as long as you want me to," Elizabeth answered.

"Well then," said Miss Stratton. "If we could just go upstairs again to see the children, then maybe we could have a nice cup of tea."

They both went back to the second floor where they found the children playing with one of the instruments. As there was only one bow that had the rosin on it, the children were taking it in turn to play. Elizabeth was slightly stunned and amazed to hear so many beautiful, clear notes. Breaking into her thoughts, the oldest girl Rachael came up to the ladies and said she thought there was some of that rosin stuff in the boxes they had found in the storeroom.

"I think you're right, Rachael," replied Miss Stratton. "Let's take another look." They rummaged round in the boxes and found the four pieces of rosin. Two pieces were light-coloured, the others darker.

"The light pieces are for the violin bows," said Elizabeth, "and the darker pieces are for the cello and the double bass." She moved over to where the bows were lying on the table. "These bows are for the violins, this one for the cello and this one for the double bass," she said, arranging them neatly. She took each bow in turn, checked the tension of the hairs, and then rubbed the correct rosin on each of them.

"So, kids," said Elizabeth, "have you decided which instruments you want to play?"

This had more or less been decided between them quite soon after they had started cleaning the instruments, so the question was very quickly answered. Grace, Evie, Freya, Jasmine and Rachael would play the violins, Zac the trumpet and Harvey had chosen the clarinet. He had been fascinated by the beautiful mechanical parts of levers and rods that operated the keys. Alexander had picked the trombone, Faith the cello because she had fallen in love with the gorgeous lustre of the colour, and Jake would play the double bass. He was quite tall and he wanted to play an instrument with deep sounds. Brandon would play lead guitar, Max the bass guitar, and Emily would play the drums.

119

"Well, that all seems to be settled," said Miss Stratton happily. "Now children," she continued, "Miss Rose and I are going downstairs for a cup of tea, but you may remain here if you want and play with the instruments. Treat them with care," she said, with sternness in her voice. "These instruments are not toys, so look after them, handle them gently and, when you have finished, make sure you put them back in the boxes properly with the bigger ones against the wall so they don't fall over. Brandon, you and Rachael make sure this happens." Having delivered her sermon, Miss Stratton relaxed and smiled.

"OK," she said, "have fun." Elizabeth and Miss Stratton left the room.

The tea was delicious and the slice of Mrs Hutchin's Victoria sponge cake was divine. Elizabeth, together with Miss Stratton, Mrs Hutchins and Miss Marigold, chatted about the recent events, the instruments, and the wonderful effect they seemed to be having on the children. Miss Marigold mentioned the record player that Elizabeth had brought with her and asked why she had brought it. Elizabeth explained and Miss Stratton exclaimed, "Could we do that now, Miss Rose? I am not that musically minded but I am so curious about this."

"Sure," replied Elizabeth. "Where would you like me to set it up?"

"We could do it in the classroom," said Miss Marigold with great excitement.

"Good," said Miss Stratton. "If you and Miss Marigold could set up the record player, I will get the children. How much Victoria sponge cake do you have, Mrs Hutchins?" she asked.

"More than enough for everyone," Mrs Hutchins replied with a grin on her face.

"Excellent Mrs Hutchins. You must join us, too. We can sit and enjoy the music, which I am sure will bring joy to our ears, especially as we will find out what Emily's little tune is all about, and we can give our taste buds a party as well," she concluded with a laugh.

Rushing upstairs, Miss Stratton went into the room where the children were with the instruments. "I would like you all to come downstairs to the classroom," she said. "I have something that I hope you will find interesting."

Eagerly, the children followed Miss Stratton down to the classroom where they immediately saw the record player.

"Are we going to listen to some music?" asked Grace, bold and impatient.

Miss Stratton turned to them.

"Now children," said Miss Stratton, "as you all are very well aware, Emily here has a habit of whistling a little tune."

"Drives us nuts," came two or three loud shouts.

Miss Stratton held up her hand. "Well, Miss Rose has kindly lent us her record player and a record of the whole piece of music that Emily keeps whistling a tiny bit of."

"And that's a really tiny bit," interrupted Jasmine loudly with a giggle.

"That will do, Jasmine," said Miss Stratton. "As I was saying," Miss Stratton continued, "Miss Rose has kindly lent us these things so that we can play this piece of music which, I am sure, you will all be very happy to hear. So, please sit down and after we have heard the music, we will all have a piece of Mrs Hutchin's delicious sponge cake." The children whooped.

Miss Stratton turned to Elizabeth and said, "Would you get things started for us please, Miss Rose?" Elizabeth opened her bag and took out a record in its cover. There was a large black and white picture of a man with swept-back hair and a slightly drooping moustache on the front.

Underneath, in gold letters edged with red, was the title and the name of the composer:

HOLBERG SUITE OP.40

EDVARD GRIEG

She placed the record on the turntable and then looked to see if everyone was ready. Adjusting the volume knob to where she thought would be a good position, she pressed the start button. As Elizabeth went to her seat, the stylus arm lifted, moved horizontally for a couple of inches, and then settled with gentle softness on the edge of the record.

Around three minutes later, the *Prelude to the Holberg Suite* ended and Elizabeth quickly got up and stopped the record player. Nobody spoke.

Evie's very quiet voice broke the silence. "Could we hear that again please, Miss?" After seeing Miss Stratton nod, Elizabeth played the record again.

When it ended, Miss Stratton said, "Well, that is what all of Emily's tune sounds like."

"It's beautiful," cried Freya, "really beautiful."

Miss Stratton looked down at Emily who was sitting beside her. The young girl was staring straight ahead, as if entranced. "Are you OK, Emily?" Miss Stratton asked, her voice like warm, soft velvet. Emily looked up at Miss Stratton and nodded. Her eyes were glistening slightly, but when she spoke her voice was clear and steady.

"I feel better now that I have heard it again," she said. "It's like my mummy's here with me again."

Chapter 12

"Before you start," she said in a calm, serious voice, "could you stand me up on that chair by the table because I have something I want to say to you all."

Rachael, who had been holding Veronica, did as she was asked.

"OK," began Veronica. "You had a little start yesterday after the man had been and fixed us all up. Because you can hear us, you won't have to go through the first difficult times that every other beginner has to go through. So, first we will teach you how to find the notes, where your fingers have to be on the fingerboard, that's this long black piece like the man told you yesterday. The next bit is up to you. You have to remember everything. You have to learn to do it without always looking. The next step will be to learn a tune. If we hear a tune, we can tell you how to play it, but that is something else you will have to sort out. We must all hear the tune otherwise we can't go any further. Hopefully, once we get all that sorted, we can learn to play together. Then we will be getting somewhere. But," she said loudly and then repeated the word again, her voice softer, "but, it isn't all going to happen overnight. When it gets to your part, remembering where to put your fingers, then things start to get tough. You will make mistakes, you'll think that you'll never remember, you'll get mad with yourselves and us, you'll feel like opening the window and throwing us out into the street." Seeing the children's heads shake "no", Veronica paused. "Yes, you will," she continued, "because everybody does. Somehow you have to get through all that, and I'll tell you how right now."

Veronica waited for a brief moment and then continued. "It's called commitment. Commitment," she repeated. "You have to really want to do this. If you don't, then you won't make it. If you're not determined, you're not being fair to your friends and we're all wasting our time. This is not a group decision decided by popular vote. It has to come from each and every one of you, individually."

"Even then, that is not the whole story," continued Veronica. "You take the beginning of a long ball of thread. The thread has no end, and it connects all the stages of your learning together and beyond. That thread has a name. It's called 'practise'. You have to keep practising, otherwise you will quickly forget some of the things you have learnt. But OK, take it a bit easy. If you start getting a bit tired of it, take a break, a day or two, but not longer. Don't force yourself to the point of opening the window." She stopped talking for a moment. "So," she continued, "Teddy and Charles are away getting fixed, so, until they are back, we won't start for proper. I've said my piece now. Think about what I have said until Teddy and Charles get back. The wind instruments can do the same for blowing techniques and the things that they do, and I'm sure Dean will do the same for the drums. Gary and Gilbert are strings, so much of what I've said applies to them as well. After we're all back together, then that will be decision time, but until then," she said, changing her tone of voice to a vibrant, laughing, joyful shout, "let's have some fun!"

They spent the next twenty minutes sorting out the bows, as each string instrument had a bow they had often worked with. The Bowie girls, together with their parents, Blake and Bella, were overjoyed to be reunited with their partners after such a long time.

"Jasmine, honey," shrieked Verity with a great peal of giggles, "push Bianca Bowie a little harder on my strings, girl, you're ticklin' me to death."

Jasmine had chosen Verity, Freya played Vivianne, Evie had taken a shine to Vera, Grace had chosen Violet and Rachael had fallen for Veronica.

"That's right," said Violet to Grace, "just move your third finger up a little bit on that string to get the note. It's a touch too low where it is now."

"You all comfy on that stool, Emily, and you guys OK standing each side by Caddie, Coral and Camilla?" asked Dean.

"I'm fine, Dean," replied Emily.

"We're good too thanks, Dean," replied Harvey and Alexander.

While Teddy and Charles were being repaired, Emily had said to the boys that they should come to the drum kit because there were more than enough drums and things for her to get to grips with all at once, and she would really appreciate a couple more pairs of hands.

"OK," said Dean. "Like I said at the beginning, with rock and roll, we lead the band, we make the beat, we're sort of in charge, but drums don't get big-headed about it. So," Dean continued, "let's hear that drum roll on the tom-toms Emily, and you boys do some soft shimmies with those light wire sticks you've got. I been wantin' to tickle up old Camilla and the twins there for a while." He finished with a big grin.

"Keep dreamin', Dean," replied Camilla with a deep chuckle and, fixing him with her twinkling blue eyes, said, "and less of the 'old' if you don't mind."

Gary, Brandon, Gilbert and Max were huddled together in a small group.

"It's like Veronica said, guys," said Gary, "we're string instruments too. You got to strum our strings with your fingers, but you got to be easy or you'll get blisters."

"We ain't got no juice either," chipped in Gilbert, "so

we ain't gonna sound so good, but you gotta learn the notes first anyway, just like any other stringed baby."

"Squeeze your lips together, Zac," said Theodore. "Then blow into my mouthpiece like you're squeezing something through a small hole. There's got to be some pressure there or I can't make any sound. Don't worry about my valves and things right now, they only change the note a bit up and down. For the basic notes you don't need the valves. You can get a lot of notes out of a bugle an' they haven't got any valves at all. Another thing, you'll need to get something to put on your lips otherwise they're gonna get awful sore."

Before they knew it, Miss Marigold was entering the room and telling them to get washed up for dinner.

During the evening meal, most of the talking was about music but they also talked about the new school that the children were going to attend.

The issue of finding a school for the children had been solved. Mr Chalmers, headmaster of the Thomas Macintyre School had been in touch and a visit to the school had been arranged. After the visit, and all the necessary paperwork had been completed, the children could restart their formal education.

When the meal was finished, Miss Stratton, Miss Marigold and Mrs Hutchins went to their sitting room. "Well ladies," said Miss Stratton, "after the activities of this last week, I'm going to have a glass of sherry. Will you join me?" Both ladies said that would be perfect. Fetching her bottle of sherry and three glasses, she poured out generous measures. Miss Stratton raised her glass and said, "To Saint Etheldreda's, and all who are here."

"To Saint Etheldreda's," chorused Miss Marigold and Mrs Hutchins before taking a large sip of the very fine liquid.

"It's wonderful to see the kids getting so involved with

this music," said Mrs Hutchins. "It seems to be making such a difference."

"Indeed, it is," agreed Miss Stratton, "and I am so very grateful for it."

They continued chatting for the rest of the evening until about nine o'clock when Miss Stratton went to see if the children were getting ready for bed. This was sometimes a bit awkward with Brandon and the older children, but it made it easier if she knew they were all in their dormitories. The older ones could read if they wanted to. Fortunately, all the beds had a little bedside lamp on the nightstand beside them.

The children had thought a little about what Veronica had said about commitment, but the younger children, were not completely sure what she meant. They knew they wanted to play the instruments and that, more or less, was that. The older ones had understood Veronica's message and explained it as best they could to the younger ones. It was the thought that was in all their heads when they finally drifted off to sleep.

Miss Stratton was speaking with Mr Robson from the Juvenile Support Department in the corridor close to the Hawk's office. She was giving him a brief update about the school she had found for the children. Then the door of the Hawk's office opened and Mr Francis, the Hawks' clerk, showed them in.

The Hawk stood up, shook their hands and then asked them to be seated. He sat down and said to the court stenographer, who was sitting at a small table, that all persons for this hearing were now assembled.

"This hearing is now in session," said the Hawk. Mr David Robson of the Juvenile Support Department and Miss Abigail Stratton of Saint Etheldreda's Foundation are present." The Hawk paused and picked up a piece of paper. Briefly scanning the page, he put it down on his desk but still held it between his fingers. Looking at Miss Stratton and Mr Robson over his half-moon glasses, he said that the investigation into the cause or causes of the fire at a previous home provided by the Juvenile Support Department of the city for children in care, had now been completed.

"Without going into technical details," the Hawk continued, "the cause of the fire was found to be a major fault in the electrical system of the building. The reasons why this fault had occurred were now being investigated further by the relevant authorities, together with the co-operation of the building owners and their contractors. No evidence whatsoever had been found to link the children to the fire and therefore the claims from the owners against the children were dismissed. The children were innocent, and the case was closed. A written confirmation of these findings will be sent to the Juvenile Support Department shortly."

The Hawk let go of the piece of paper he was holding and leant back in his chair and at the same time Miss Stratton let out a long, deep sigh of relief. The Hawk's lips widened, his cheeks blossomed out and his eyes narrowed slightly and twinkled. His face showed to Miss Stratton that he totally understood her rather noisy reaction. Sitting up straight again, the Hawk said, "Now, please tell me what is the situation at the Foundation. How are things progressing?"

"Well, Your Honour," Miss Stratton replied, "the children and the staff are settling in very well, the children have restarted school this week at a very nice local school, and they have also found some activities that are keeping them occupied." She did not mention anything about musical instruments.

"Excellent," replied the Hawk. Turning to the stenographer

he said that the court business was now concluded and she was free to go. After she had left the room, the Hawk continued speaking. "There is one other matter I would like to inform you about." he said. "I am in the process of retiring. I have been working in the Juvenile Court for some years now and I have come to the conclusion that I would like to remain involved in the general wellbeing of children in care, but following a different path. Therefore, I would like you to know that I wish to offer any service that I can provide to the Support Department, on a voluntary basis, in any way that can be helpful to you." He then gave Miss Stratton and Mr Robson a card with his name, private address and telephone number printed on it.

"That is extremely kind of you, Your Honour," replied Mr Robson. "I will inform the Department of your offer and I'm sure we will be in contact with you soon."

They all stood and the Hawk shook their hands. As they were leaving the room, the Hawk asked if he might have a quick word with Miss Stratton. Miss Stratton and Mr Robson said their goodbyes. After Mr Robson had gone, the Hawk said that he would very much like to keep contact with the Foundation and follow its progress. Whether that was due to the fact that this was his last case or not he did not know. Miss Stratton replied that she would be delighted to keep him informed of everything that was going on.

On her way back to Saint Etheldreda's, Miss Stratton began to realise that the Hawk had many similar characteristics to the man she had so deeply loved long ago and who had been tragically been taken from her.

Arriving back at Saint Etheldreda's, Miss Stratton had immediately told Miss Marigold and Mrs Hutchins what had happened at the Juvenile Court that morning.

"Oh, what a great relief," said Miss Marigold with a huge sigh. "The children will be so happy to hear that."

"Wonderful news, Miss Stratton," said Mrs Hutchins. "That must be a great load off your mind."

"You can say that again, Mrs Hutchins," said Miss Stratton with huge sigh.

Sitting at her desk that afternoon, Miss Stratton received a telephone call from Elizabeth to say that Mario and his sons had completed the repairs to the clarinet and trombone. They would like to return them to Saint Etheldreda's the following morning. Elizabeth also said she would like to come to the Foundation this coming Saturday in the afternoon for a couple of hours between two and four o'clock if that was OK. When the children had arrived back from school, Miss Stratton had gathered them in the TV room and told them the news from the court.

"We told them that we didn't do anything," said Brandon.

"Well, it's all over now so you can forget all about it," said Miss Stratton. Changing the subject, she asked if they had any homework to do that day. With varying groans, they all said they had, so Miss Stratton told them it would be good if they could go to the classroom and get that done before dinner.

"If you get all your homework done, then I may have some other news for you," said Miss Stratton with a tantalising smile. The children scurried off to the classroom.

"Don't rush your food," said Miss Stratton firmly, "and I hope you did not hurtle through your homework, either," she added, trying to keep a straight face.

The children were eager, impatient and excited. They wanted to know what Miss Stratton's news was. They finished their meal and did the washing up and other chores in record-setting time.

"Off you go to the TV room," said Miss Stratton. "We will be there in a moment."

The children were all gathered in the TV room when Miss Stratton and Miss Marigold entered.

"I'm sure you will all be pleased to know, especially you Harvey and you Alexander, that tomorrow the repaired instruments will come back to us from Mr Rozetti. Harvey and Alexander grinned.

"So," continued Miss Stratton, "on that happy note—" she suddenly stopped when Miss Marigold started giggling and, realising her choice of words. She laughed before continuing, "On that happy note," she repeated, "we will leave you in peace for a while."

After Miss Stratton and Miss Marigold had left the room, Brandon turned to the children. "Everybody thought about what Veronica told us about commitment?" he asked them. "Everybody sure they really want to start on this?"

"Could you maybe explain what she really meant, Brandon," said Emily. "I didn't really understand all of it." Grace and Jasmine were happy that Emily had asked this question as they were not completely sure what Veronica had meant either.

Brandon explained what Veronica had said using words that Emily could follow. Nodding slowly as he spoke, Emily began to understand. When he had finished, Emily said, "So if we start, we have to keep going," she said. "We can't just do it when we feel like it as a sort of game, but we can have fun right?"

"Sure, we can have fun," said Brandon. "They want us to have fun, but we can't learn how to play them for a week here and there, and then forget about it for months. We have to practise every day unless we really get fed up. "So," he continued, "are we all OK with that?" They all nodded; their faces serious and determined.

131

"OK," continued Brandon. "Let's all make a promise to each other." The children knelt on the floor in a circle. Brandon put his right hand, palm down, on the floor, and each child put their right hand on top of the person next to them. All together, they promised they would not quit; they would all see it through.

The doorbell rang and the twinkling face of Mario Rozetti beamed at Miss Stratton as she opened the door.

"Forgive me, Madame," he said, taking her hand and kissing the back of it, in a way that Miss Stratton thought had ended in the last century, but which gave her an enormous thrill, "I have to go shopping urgently with my wife," he explained. "Seems another little bambino will be with us soon," he continued, "and my wife needs to buy something urgently, so I cannot stay long." He picked up two packages, which were obviously the trombone and the clarinet and said the instruments had been repaired and were now ready for use. He asked where he should put them, and Miss Stratton said to place them against the wall in the hall and she would have them taken up to the second floor straightaway.

"I cannot thank you enough, Mr Rozetti," said Miss Stratton, "and by the way, many congratulations to you and your wife," she continued with a delighted smile. "You must rush now and not keep your wife waiting," she said. Mario Rozetti quickly kissed Miss Stratton's hand again and rushed down the steps.

Miss Stratton saw Max on his way to the TV room and she asked him if he and Brandon would kindly take the repaired instruments up to the second floor, which they did.

That afternoon, Elizabeth arrived at the Foundation.

"Why hello, Miss Rose," said Miss Stratton with a cheerful face. "Your friend Mr Rozetti brought the two instruments, which he has repaired, back to us this morning. A charming man and I am so glad you introduced us to him and got him to do this work. I really can never thank you enough. I had a very quick look at the instruments myself just now, and they look better than new," she concluded.

"Believe me, Miss Stratton," answered Elizabeth gaily, "the pleasure is all his and mine."

"Well," continued Miss Stratton, "the children are just finishing the washing up but you are welcome to go up to the second floor and see the repaired instruments, or would you rather a cup of tea first?"

"No tea thank you, Miss Stratton, so if it's OK I would like to go upstairs," Elizabeth replied.

"Whatever you wish, my dear," replied Miss Stratton, "but do pop in to our sitting room before you go." Elizabeth promised to do so. There was nobody in the room when Elizabeth arrived, so she went to inspect the trombone and clarinet that had been unwrapped and were lying on one of the tables. Mario and his sons had made a beautiful job, and Elizabeth mentally agreed with Miss Stratton that they looked better than new. She was still admiring the craftsmanship when the children arrived in the room.

"Hello, Miss Rose," they said with genuine pleasure at seeing her there.

"Hello," she replied to each of them by name, as she now remembered them all. "As I hope to see you all often," she continued, "you may call me Miss Elizabeth. She told them to get some chairs from the stack against the wall and put them in a semi-circle. The children went and picked up their instruments and, apart from Jake with Danny the double bass, they all sat down. Emily seated herself on her drum stool. Harvey and Alexander did not join her this time as now that the trombone and the clarinet had been repaired, they all had instruments.

"OK," she said, "show me what you can do."

One by one, they all got started and began playing a whole selection of notes. The combined sounds were chaotic.

"Wait a minute," Elizabeth cried out above the din. "We need to do this another way." Thinking furiously, she came up with an idea.

"I will sing out a note and you all see if you can play it," she said. She sang out a note she thought was middle "C". The children played the note they had heard, and Elizabeth's chin bounced off the floor, her mouth wide open, and her astonished eyes were staring in disbelief. The note that the children had played was almost perfect.

"Was that OK, Miss Elizabeth?" asked Rachael.

Gathering her wits together, Elizabeth replied, "My goodness, that was truly amazing."

"Now try this," she said, and she sang out four notes rising up the scale. Elizabeth focused on Harvey with the clarinet. She knew this was the first time he had ever picked up the instrument. He was just sitting, doing nothing, but he appeared to be listening to something. She kept looking. She saw him moving his mouth as if to find the right position to blow, then his fingers went to the levers which operated the keys. All this took a second or two, then he played the first note, which at first sounded strangled, but then became strong and perfectly in tune. Elizabeth felt the hairs rising on her neck. This was incredible. This was beyond understanding. She switched her attention back to the other instruments just in time to hear them play the last flawless note. She sang four more different notes and moved her eyes to Alexander. He was standing with the trombone moving his lips and then moving the slide. The series of notes that followed were faultless.

Six more notes came from Elizabeth's beautiful voice

and she looked at the girls playing the violins. It was the same. They were placing their fingers on the strings and then moving them slightly up or down before drawing the bow over them. All the notes they played were perfect. Elizabeth's throat was as dry as dust. She found herself gripping the chair as if her life depended on it; her stomach was knotted and her tongue stuck to the top of her mouth. She was transfixed.

"So, what d'ya think, Miss Elizabeth?" called out Grace, who had stopped playing. "Are we doin' OK? You OK, Miss Elizabeth?" she continued. "You've gone a funny colour."

"That was wonderful, Grace," Elizabeth somehow managed to croak. "Play the last lot of notes again for me." Grace played the notes again.

Throughout this time, Emily had been sitting, softly tapping the drums with her drumsticks. She was feeling a bit left out until Elizabeth, noticing her unsmiling face, called out, "OK, Emily. It's your turn. Let's see what you can do." Emily's face changed to a big grin and she started to make some quite complicated drum rolls, finishing off with a hard bang on the cymbal. With the same incredulous expression on her face, Elizabeth showered praise on Emily's performance with gasps of intense surprise.

The chaos in Elizabeth's mind slowly calmed; she started to relax, her muscles lost their tenseness and she regained control of her knees and tongue. For reasons she could not even explain to herself, it crept into her mind that she did not need to know how or why. If these children had been given a gift, she did not need to understand it. If that is what they had been given, then it filled her with an overwhelming joy. She managed to stand up, and with all her normal bodily senses rapidly returning, she flew around the room like a mother hen showering praise on her chicks.

"If you will excuse me for a moment, kids," she said, "I just need to go and ask Miss Stratton something." She left the room and was nearly at the first floor when she almost bumped into Miss Marigold and Miss Stratton who were about to start coming up the stairs.

"Oh, hello Miss Rose," said Miss Marigold. "We were just coming up to see you, to see what was going on."

"Oh, ladies," exclaimed Elizabeth. "The children. It's remarkable what they have managed to learn in just one week. It's truly amazing."

"Really," replied Miss Stratton somewhat surprised. "I don't know how, I'm sure, but if they have, then they have. Shall we continue up?" she asked.

"Oh yes, of course," replied Elizabeth, and they all walked up to the second floor.

Once in the room, Elizabeth repeated the note she previously sang, so Miss Stratton and Miss Marigold could hear them play.

"That's terrific," chimed Miss Stratton and Miss Marigold almost together.

"You must be so pleased with yourselves," added Miss Marigold. Turning to Elizabeth she continued, "Isn't this exciting? Who would have thought that this could happen?"

Elizabeth agreed that some marvellous things were developing, but at the same time a problem came into her mind that she knew she had to fix, and she had to fix it fast.

Chapter 13

The finishing line was in sight. Her legs and feet begging for rest were ignored. Mentally thanking herself for not wearing high-heeled shoes, Elizabeth Rose arrived at the Music Shop and was overjoyed to find it was still open.

The Music Shop had recently started to sell tape recorders, and Elizabeth went to the section of the shop where they were displayed. After a few minutes, a keen sales assistant asked her if she needed any help. Elizabeth gratefully accepted, as she knew nothing about tape recorders at all. He asked her what type of tape recorder she was looking for, and she replied that it needed to be something portable. The sales assistant led her to the other end of the display. There, Elizabeth saw some very small machines she thought would be ideal.

The sales assistant began to explain that these recorders had fewer possibilities, had very small control buttons, and had small tape spools which reduced the playing time.

"For their size, they are quite expensive," said the assistant, "but that's due to the costs of making such small parts. They do, however, have the advantage of being able to operate on both batteries and mains power," he concluded.

"How much are they?" Elizabeth asked. Her heart sank when she heard the prices. "The reason I need a tape recorder is so I can record a few tunes for a project I am involved with," she said to the sales assistant. "Normally, I would have done this with my own piano, but I don't have one at the moment. So, I was wondering if I could use one of your pianos for a few minutes now and then so I can make some recordings? If I can't do that, then there is not much point in buying a tape recorder," she concluded.

Hesitating for a moment, the sales assistant replied,

"Just a moment ma'am, I will go and ask the manager." A few minutes later, the sales assistant returned with the manager.

"Good afternoon, ma'am," the manager began. "My assistant informs me that you have asked if you can use one of our pianos from time to time and, if that was possible, that you would then purchase one of our small tape recorders."

"That's correct," Elizabeth replied.

"Quite so, ma'am, quite so," purred the manager. "Maybe you would like to follow me, ma'am," he said, and he led her to the area of the shop where the pianos were displayed. He stopped in front of an instrument that was definitely second hand, yet still in very nice condition.

"If you would like to try this piano," said the manager, "to see if the sound is to your liking?"

Elizabeth had the sneaking feeling that the manager was checking to see if she could actually play the piano and in this, she was absolutely right. Elizabeth treated the manager and the sales assistant to part of a captivating melody, then sat back and smiled. The manager, in a voice that had lost its superior tone and taken on real sincerity, said she had played the piece absolutely beautifully.

"Well now," continued the manager, still sounding sincere, "if you could come early on the days you wish to play, as soon as the shop opens at eight thirty when it is usually very quiet, I do not think there will be any problem at all for you to make your recordings, if that would be satisfactory for you, ma'am."

"That would be perfect, and thank you so much for your help, sir," replied Elizabeth, giving him a gleaming smile. "If I may, could I come tomorrow morning?"

"Certainly, ma'am," replied the manager. "I look forward to seeing you then."

The manager then returned to his office, leaving his assistant to complete the sale of the tape recorder to Elizabeth.

"We have these recorders all packed up in our stock room, ma'am," the sales assistant said. "These ones here are for display purposes only, so if you would like to come over to the sales desk and complete the purchase, I will get the machine for you straightaway." Elizabeth made out a cheque and handed it to the assistant.

Elizabeth went to the Music Shop every morning that week from half past eight until ten minutes to nine to record single note tunes with no chords that she made up in her head. She had to leave then and rush to her office to start work at half past nine. Even though she was only in the shop for twenty minutes at a time, she was quick at what she was doing, so that by the time she left the shop on Friday morning, she had enough tunes to make a start. The fact that the tape recorder operated on batteries was a major advantage.

She arrived at Saint Etheldreda's at just after two o'clock the following Sunday afternoon and, after greeting Miss Stratton, Miss Marigold and Mrs Hutchins, she went upstairs to the music room.

"Hello, kids," she said brightly. They watched her take the little tape recorder out of her bag, put it on one of the tables, and plug it into the nearby electric socket. The children gathered around the tape recorder and with excitement and curiosity, they asked her questions about it.

"OK, kids," said Elizabeth, "today we are going to start something different, the next stage if you like. We are going to start playing proper tunes." She told them to arrange their chairs around the tape recorder so they could all hear it properly as, being such a small machine, it was not all that loud, even when on its highest volume. Elizabeth explained what she was going to do and then pressed the play button on the tape. The children listened intently and after the first tune was finished, Elizabeth rewound the tape and played the tune again. She did this three times and then said, "OK, everyone got the tune in their heads?"

They all nodded, and then Emily piped up, "But what do I do?"

Elizabeth said to Emily that she would sit next to her and tell her when to do a little drum roll and when to hit the cymbals while the others played the tune.

"OK, ready?" asked Elizabeth. The children all nodded again and were obviously eager to start. "OK," Elizabeth continued. "Emily will start with a drum roll, and then I want everybody to try to play the tune." They started, and the first attempt was shambolic. Most of the notes were right, but they were everything except together. At the end, the children all started laughing and Elizabeth joined in.

"OK," said Elizabeth, "try it again." After they had played it four or five times, they were playing the tune without any mistakes and pretty well together.

"That's great," exclaimed Elizabeth, still amazed by how quickly they had mastered it. "Let's try another tune now." Going to the tape recorder, she repeated the exercise with the next tune she had recorded at the Music Shop. It took a little longer with the second tune as it was a little more complicated, but after about half an hour, they were playing it really well. By this time, it was about fifteen minutes to four. Elizabeth declared, "That's enough for today." She then suggested they all go down to the kitchen, and the kids could tell her about how things were going at school.

While the children had been playing their instruments upstairs, Miss Stratton had been sitting at her desk writing

140

a rather formal report to the Hawk about all the recent activities. His real name was Mr Peter Riley, so she started the report with "Dear Mr Riley". After writing as much as she wished, she put it in an envelope, sealed it, and left it on her desk ready for posting. Leaning back in her chair, Miss Stratton once again reflected on the similarities between the Hawk and the man she had loved. Originally, she had intended to write to the Hawk about once a month, but now she thought she would do so every week, thinking it would be good to get to know him better. She was not interested in anything romantic, but it would be nice to be able to talk with someone of around her own age for a change.

The sands of time moved quickly through the busy days of the week and, once again, Elizabeth was standing in the room on the second floor of Saint Etheldreda's Foundation. She had recorded more tunes at the Music Shop and was playing the recorder to the children to make a start.

Then Evie piped up, "Can you play that again please, Miss Elizabeth? Vera missed some of it." The words were no sooner out of Evie's mouth than she turned bright red and looked at the floor.

"Who's Vera, Evie?" asked Elizabeth in a gentle tone. Evie kept staring at the floor and said nothing. "It's OK Evie, I won't laugh," said Elizabeth, in a coaxing voice.

"Vera's my violin," Evie whispered.

"Why, that's really nice of you to give your violin a name," said Elizabeth. "It's like having a best friend. Does anyone else have a name for their instrument?" she asked with genuine interest. One by one, the children told Elizabeth the names of their instruments; some with open pride, others slightly embarrassed. Elizabeth quickly went to her handbag, took out a piece of paper and a pen, and after asking them the names again, wrote down the child's and the instrument's name together on a list. They then went back to playing the musical notes game with Elizabeth, realising that the more complicated some of the recordings were, the more times she had to repeat them before the children got it. They played the game until around four o'clock, when Elizabeth thought they had probably had enough.

The moon had travelled a complete circle around the earth, and Elizabeth had gone to Saint Etheldreda's four more times. It was during her last visit that she sensed something was changing. She did not know exactly what it was until Grace made it plain.

"When are we going to do something else, Miss Elizabeth?" she had asked. "This is getting a bit boring."

Shocked, Elizabeth understood that the children's interest was slowing. She needed to find something to keep the flame alive, but she had no idea what. All she knew was that if the children stopped playing because of her, she would never forgive herself.

Chapter 14

"What on earth is this, Lizzie?" said Stephen Hanney. "You've missed out half of this form altogether."

Elizabeth looked up; a confused expression on her face., Her mind had been elsewhere.

"Sorry, Stephen. What did you just say? Have I forgotten something?" she said.

"These last few days, Lizzie," said Stephen, "you seem to be thinking of something else, and it is affecting your normally superb work. Are you worried about something? Is there anything I can help you with? I have hidden talents you know," he continued, "but I admit they are all so well hidden that I have not found any of them yet." He finished with a laugh to lighten the mood. Elizabeth laughed and said that maybe today would be his lucky day. She then became serious again as she thought about what she was going to say. Having decided that it would do no harm, she began to tell him about what was happening with her voluntary work at the Foundation. She explained the situation she was now struggling with.

"That sounds tricky," Stephen replied, "but I'll search around to see if I have a talent to fix it."

Smiling, Elizabeth poked her tongue out at him and then wished she hadn't. She continued working up until lunchtime and then took a break, walking aimlessly around the nearby streets, the problem taking over her entire mind.

Returning to her desk, she resumed her work. Twenty minutes later, Stephen also returned to the office and instead of sitting at his desk, he perched himself on the corner of Elizabeth's.

"What do you think of this, Lizzie?" he said before explaining his idea to her.

Elizabeth rang the doorbell, and Miss Marigold opened it a few moments later.

"Oh, what a surprise to see you on a Wednesday evening, Miss Rose," said Miss Marigold. "Please come in."

"Is Miss Stratton in please, Miss Marigold?" asked Elizabeth. "There is something I need to talk to her about."

"I think she's in her office," said Miss Marigold. She led Elizabeth to Miss Stratton's door. Knocking, Miss Marigold heard, "Come in please," and both she and Elizabeth entered. Miss Stratton was also surprised to see Elizabeth on a weekday and asked if everything was OK.

"I hope so Miss Stratton," answered Elizabeth, "but there is something I want to talk to you about."

"Please sit down, my dear," replied Miss Stratton, "and tell us what is on your mind." After she and Miss Marigold were seated, Elizabeth explained the idea Stephen Hanney had come up with and what she wanted to do.

"Before I even start on this," said Elizabeth, "I want to know how you feel about it, if I have your permission, and if you think it would be OK for the children to do it." Miss Stratton did not answer immediately, but sat in concentrated thought.

"Well," she said finally, "it would certainly be different. You would first need to see the reaction from the children. If they want to do it, then I cannot see any objection. We may have to check on any legal aspects of your idea, but as far as I can see, it rests with the children. If they are OK with it, then so am I. What's your opinion, Miss Marigold?" asked Miss Stratton.

"I think it's the best idea I have heard in a long, long time," Miss Marigold answered.

"How about a cup of tea, Miss Rose," said Miss Stratton, "then we can ask Mrs Hutchins' opinion."

The three of them went to the kitchen and Elizabeth explained the plan to Mrs Hutchins. She thought it was a capital idea, but agreed with Miss Stratton that the children had to make the final choice, as they were the ones who would have to carry it out. If they did not want to do it, then it was not going to happen.

"Are the kids going to be here all through the summer holidays, Miss Stratton?" Elizabeth asked.

"Not all of them, Miss Rose. Some of them are going away with other children from the school for ten days, starting the week after the holidays begin. It's something the headmaster Mr Chalmers arranges every year."

"I see," said Elizabeth. "Well, if it happens at all, it would be best to do it before they go away, otherwise they will forget things. That gives us about six weeks, including this one. I need to try and fix the first part of the idea as soon as possible. Hopefully, I can manage that, so that leaves us with about five weeks."

"Is that enough time?" asked Mrs Hutchins. "It seems very short to me."

"I think they can do it, Mrs Hutchins." Elizabeth thought about the amazing gift the children had. "OK," continued Elizabeth brightly. "I will get started on the first part and then go on from there. Finishing her tea, Elizabeth left the Foundation. She knew that she had to succeed. It was the only way she could keep her new picture alive.

Dashing from the door of her apartment without taking off her shoes and coat, Elizabeth picked up her telephone and dialled the number she wanted. After three rings, the telephone connected and Elizabeth heard the lilting voice of an Italian lady.

"Hello, Maria," said Elizabeth. "It's been a while since we last talked."

"Elizabeth," cried Maria, her light voice full of welcoming surprise. "How are you? Lovely to hear you again."

Elizabeth had only met Maria twice before, but they had instantly clicked with each other on both occasions.

"Is Mario at home please, Maria," Elizabeth asked.

"He here," answered Maria. "A momen' an' I will get 'im for you."

After a moment of silence, Elizabeth heard Mario's voice in her ear.

"Hello, Mario," she said. "Sorry to trouble you at home, but something urgent has come up and I need a lot of help."

"What you need?" Mario asked.

Elizabeth explained her colleague, Stephen's idea. There was silence for a few moments before Mario responded. "I don't know if I can help you with this, Elizabeth, but I will talk with the family to see if they can help. Maybe give me a call tomorrow evening and I will be able to tell you more."

Standing with fraying nerves in her manager's office with her holiday request form in her hand, Elizabeth began the next part of the plan. When he had finished writing, he looked up at Elizabeth and smiled. "What can I do for you, Miss Rose?" he said.

"I need to take two or three days' holiday this week starting tomorrow," Elizabeth said coming straight to the point. "I know I have only been here a short time and that I have not really earned these days off," she continued quickly, "but it is very important to me. I do not make this request lightly."

The manager's face was grave. "You know the policy about holidays, Miss Rose," he replied, "but as I have come to know you a little over the time you have been here, I am prepared to listen to the reasons you are asking for this time off at such short notice."

Elizabeth knew she had to be totally honest and tell him

146

everything. She told him about her voluntary work at Saint Etheldreda's Foundation, and the situation she was now in. Her manager listened intently and, after she had finished her explanation, he remained silent, reflecting on her words.

"Your work is very noble," he eventually said. "May I take this information further, in confidence of course?" he asked.

"Certainly," Elizabeth replied.

"Come back at the end of the day and I hope by then to give you your answer." The day seemed to last forever; she concentrated hard on her work, hoping to make it pass more quickly. Just before five o'clock, she went back to her manager's office.

"Please close the door and sit down, Miss Rose," he said. "Well, I have spoken about this situation to my superiors and we are in agreement. We find your request acceptable and will allow you to take this holiday."

"Oh, thank you so much," Elizabeth burst out. "I am immensely grateful."

"Not at all, Miss Rose," he replied. "We found your reasons very touching. They are not for your own benefit but for the benefit of others who, due to their circumstances, deserve the things you are trying to do for them. We will also be flexible with any future time off you may need to complete this project, provided it does not impact on the work of the department." He did not tell her that his superior had discussed her holiday request with Mr Robson in the Juvenile Support Department, who had stressed the value of her transformative work. "But," he added with a half-smile, "please try to follow the rules next time."

"Oh, I will," replied Elizabeth, and she left the room with one hurdle overcome.

At the time Mario had given her as the best time to call, Elizabeth dialled the number.

"Well," Mario began. "I talked with the family and maybe we 'ave a solution."

Elizabeth listened tensely, hanging on to every word.

"My daughter, Rosa, is married to a man who work' in the advertising business," continued Mario. "She talked to 'im about your problem and it seems that 'is company use another small company, which mainly employ musicians, to make background music and jingle' for their advertisements. My son in-law say to maybe contact them. You can use my son in-law name if you wan'." Mario gave his son in-law's name, which was Paul Henderson, together with the musicians' company details and a contact name.

"Oh Mario," gushed Elizabeth. "Thank you so much. It is at least a start and maybe even the solution." After a few minutes further chatting, with Mario wishing Elizabeth the best of luck, they hung up.

Elizabeth had far too much energy pumping around her to sleep. Instead, she prepared herself for the next day by running what she wanted through her mind to make sure she had not forgotten anything. Lying in her bed with her arms behind her head, she stared at the white ceiling above her, using it as a blank canvas to picture her plans. At some point, she must have dozed off as she woke with a start to the noise of her alarm clock. Springing out of her bed, she got herself ready for the day and, after hurriedly eating a slice of toast and gulping down a cup of coffee, she put on her shoes, grabbed her coat, and hurried to the bus stop. Arriving sometime later at the bus station, she studied the routes and bus numbers that would take her to the address Mario had given her. She had to wait as patiently as she could for nearly twenty minutes before the bus she needed arrived.

Now she stood in front of a building in a more industrial

part of the city. Her stomach clenched with nerves; she was uncertain in the unfamiliar surroundings. This was the main obstacle. If the people in this building could not help her, then she did not want to think about the impact. She felt stupid, wishing she had made an appointment instead of acting on unthinking impulse. She approached the bright-coloured door and walked into a nicely furnished reception area.

"Good morning," said a middle-aged lady in a kind voice. "How may I help you?"

"I'm sorry to have barged in like this," began Elizabeth. "I should have called you to maybe make an appointment."

"That's OK," replied the receptionist. "If you tell me who you are and what it is you are looking for, then I will see how I can help you."

"Oh yes, sorry," Elizabeth flustered. "My name is Elizabeth Rose, and I was told to speak with a gentleman named Joe. I have the name of this company and Joe's name from a Mr Paul Henderson."

"Oh, we know Mr Henderson well," said the lady. "He is quite a large client of ours. Just give me a moment and I will see if Joe is available."

Five minutes later, Elizabeth found herself in an alien world of electrical hardware, tape recorders, record players and an army of other unknown equipment. It was like a set from a science fiction movie. She and Joe introduced themselves to each other and Elizabeth made comments about the contents of the room and how strange they were to her eyes, which darted about, taking in the wonders of Joe's domain.

Joe began to ask her exactly what it was that he could help her with. She started to explain the situation where she had thirteen instruments, thirteen children who could not read music but somehow managed to pick up tunes by

149

listening to them, and she wanted to create something special for them based on this piece of music. She pulled the record out of her bag.

"Well," said Joe. "First of all, what instruments do you have?" Elizabeth gave him the details.

"So," continued Joe, "if I understand you correctly, you want a new piece of music composed on the basis of this piece." He paused, pointing at the record Elizabeth was holding, "And then you need separate sound tracks for each instrument or group of the same or similar instruments so that the players can learn their individual tunes from listening to the soundtrack."

"Yes," replied Elizabeth simply.

Joe blew out his cheeks and replied, laughing, "You don't want much then do you?"

Elizabeth was glad that Joe had laughed as it gave her some sort of hope.

"OK," said Joe. "It is possible, but it will take time. How big is the tape recorder you have and how long does one spool play for?" She put her hand in her bag and took out the instruction book she had brought with her, and gave it to him. He studied it for a few minutes and wrote down some details on his pad. He also noted the name of the Music Shop from their sticker on the front. "OK," he continued, "I have all the info I need should I have to get more blank tapes. In case all this goes ahead, I would like to make a quick recording of the piece you want us to work with so that you won't have to come all the way back here." He took the record from Elizabeth's hand, got up, and walked to a collection of equipment. Fifteen minutes later, the recording was done, and he handed the record back to Elizabeth.

"Now I'll have to run all this by my boss," Joe replied, "and he can decide if we can do this for sure and what it will cost you."

150

"OK," she replied. "When do you think you will be able to tell me?"

"When do you need all this for?" Joe asked.

"Yesterday," Elizabeth replied.

"I'm a sound engineer not a magician," Joe replied, laughing. "Give me your telephone number and I will try to get back to you tonight, providing my boss lets me get started right away."

They shook hands and Joe took her back to the reception area where Elizabeth also said goodbye to the kind receptionist. She then made her way back to the city shopping complex and spent time wandering around various shops impatiently killing time for a few hours. By three o'clock in the afternoon, she was back in her apartment waiting with jangling nerves for Joe to call. At just after half past four, the telephone rang and Elizabeth eagerly picked it up. It was Joe.

"OK," he began. "I talked to my boss about all the things you require and we reckon we can do it."

Elizabeth felt her hopes soaring. She was going to do it. This was going to work. At last, this was something worthwhile that she was going to achieve. The new picture of this next chapter in her life was going to be bright, full of hope and happiness. Then Joe told her what it would cost. He heard the sharp intake of breath.

"Sorry, Elizabeth, but that's the best we can do," he said.

"Well, thanks for all your help anyway, Joe," Elizabeth replied in a stunned voice. "I will be in touch one way or another by the end of the week." She put the telephone down.

Holding her face in her hands, she knew she could never find that sort of money. She had already spent a large part of her small savings on the little tape recorder. Paying her rent and all the other necessary bills during the time when she had no job had taken her to the brink of homelessness. She desperately needed to talk to someone. Picking up the telephone, she called the Foundation. After speaking briefly with Miss Marigold, Elizabeth was soon talking to Miss Stratton, telling her about what had happened that day. Miss Stratton was silent. The seconds ticked by.

"I am deeply sorry, Elizabeth," Miss Stratton said, "but I'm afraid we will have to forget all about it."

Sitting with her legs curled beneath her on her sofa, Elizabeth stared at nothing. Her balloon of euphoria, filled only yesterday with ecstasy, had exploded, and the wreckage now fell with increasing speed towards the black hole, the inescapable vortex of despair that captured her so often and so easily. The added weight of guilt, knowing the disappointment of the children and the embarrassment she would face with her manager at work was too much. Drained and despondent, she craved for the oblivion of sleep. Going to her bathroom, she opened the mirrored cabinet, and took out the nearly full bottle of sleeping pills. She filled the glass on the wash basin, unscrewed the top of the bottle and shook a pill out into her hand. Usually, one sleeping pill was enough. She looked at the pill lying in her hand for a moment, then shook the bottle again and added two more. Elizabeth put the three pills into her mouth, took a large sip of water from the glass, and swallowed them. Closing the cabinet, she looked into the mirror. Gazing at her reflection, silent words came back to her.

You are useless. You cannot make a success of anything. Nobody will miss you as you only let them down. You fail at everything so you may as well give up now as it won't get any better... She looked down at the bottle. Impulsively, she poured all the pills into her hand.

Chapter 15

"No, Peter," Miss Stratton cried out, seeing what it was he had in his hand. "That I cannot accept."

The need to talk had been crushing, so she had called the Hawk the evening before to talk about the situation. The weekly correspondence between them had quickly become a much more informal, chatty communication to the point where they were now on first-name terms. The Hawk had replied to Miss Stratton's letters from the start. Now, after a tour of the Foundation, he sat in her office.

"It's not your decision to make," said the Hawk very firmly. "I can understand that you may feel too proud," he continued bluntly, "but don't let that cause you to lose sight of where you are trying to go; what you are trying to achieve. It is not about me or you, Abigail, it's about the children. The rest is of secondary importance." The Hawk paused. "As a judge," he continued, "I had to remain impartial, only involved from a legal perspective. I could not form any personal attachment, but now I have retired, I am free from such rules. Since my dear wife passed away, I have led a quiet life. Now I have the opportunity to do something constructive; to get involved with something worthwhile; to become part of something. You would not wish to deny me that, would you, Abigail?" he concluded with eyebrows raised.

Miss Stratton shook her head. Her defiant eyes mellowed. She knew he was right.

"I'm sorry, Peter," she said. "You are right. The priority is the children."

"Well then, Abigail, let us go onward together on this particular journey," said the Hawk. Using the information she had provided, two cheques were soon in Miss Stratton's

153

hand. Putting them in her desk drawer, she reached for her telephone.

The shrill noise of the telephone was ignored. She did not move. The ringing stopped.

Moments later, the telephone began its strident call again. Elizabeth closed her hand around the pills and shuffled reluctantly towards the intrusive noise. She picked up the handset.

"Hello," she said, her tone flat and indifferent. "Hello, Elizabeth," said Miss Stratton. Then after a short pause she said, "Are you all right Elizabeth?"

Sighing with the pointlessness of the question, Elizabeth replied in a dull tone, "Yes."

"Well, good news," continued Miss Stratton. "The difficulty we found ourselves in yesterday has been solved. So could you please contact the music company you visited yesterday and tell them we accept their offer and would like to go ahead? Isn't that good news, Elizabeth?" Miss Stratton concluded.

Elizabeth said nothing. She couldn't care less anymore. The pills in her hand were her comfort.

"Elizabeth, are you still there?" came the concerned voice of Miss Stratton.

The words Elizabeth heard entered another part of her mind. It was no longer anything to do with her. It did not matter anymore, but she would do this one last thing.

"Could you repeat what you just said please, Miss Stratton," Elizabeth said, "just in case I misunderstood you?" Miss Stratton repeated her message.

"OK, Miss Stratton," Elizabeth said and she ended the call. She then dialled a number.

"Hello, Joe," she said, sounding far away. "We can go ahead. We can accept your proposal."

"That's great," Joe replied. "I will tell my boss and try to get started with everything today. I'll try to get it all done by the end of the week. It will be tight, but we will really try," Joe said. "Tell you what I will do," continued Joe. "I will give you a call tomorrow with an update."

"OK, Joe," said Elizabeth before hanging up. The abrupt ending of the call took Joe by surprise.

Opening her hand, she looked at the pills and then closed her fingers around them. Enough was enough. No more disappointments, no more heartaches. She went back to her bathroom and stared again into the mirror. Her fingers tightened around the pills; her teeth clamped. This was the moment, but she could not move. Elizabeth closed her eyes and an image of thirteen children flashed before her. She tried to block it from her mind but she couldn't. The image was too powerful. It was a message from her heart: she must not take the final step. The muscles in her hand rebelled, her fingers dropped open, and the sleeping pills fell to the floor.

The cauldron of burning pain inside her surged upwards like molten lava, and erupted as hot, stinging tears through her aching eyes. With choking gasps, a strangled cry of desolation escaped from her constricted throat. Elizabeth sank to the floor and curled herself into a ball. She lay there for a long time.

Her body twitched, and then the pain in her shoulder, elbow and hip brought consciousness. Her eyelids were sticky and it was hard to open her eyes. With blurred vision, she gazed at the floor, not understanding where she was. Her lips, mouth and throat were dry, and she moved her wooden tongue over the roof of her mouth, trying to make saliva. Some far-off ringing sound entered her dazed mind, but she couldn't make out what it was. Trying to move, every

155

muscle aching, she pushed herself up, but her legs buckled, so she began to crawl, each movement bringing pain to her stiff joints. Dragging herself forward, she inched towards her sitting room, and the ringing sound in her ears got louder. She was halfway across the room when the ringing stopped. Her head turned in slow motion as she gazed around the unfamiliar room in a dreamlike state. She took long, deep breaths, trying to make sense of what she saw. The ringing started again and she crawled towards the sound. Putting her hands on the table, she pulled herself up onto her knees, and with fumbling, trembling hands, she picked up the receiver.

"Hi, Elizabeth," said Joe as Elizabeth held the receiver to her ear. "Well, we have made a start, and I have recorded some music based on the tune and style that you wanted. So, if you could come around tomorrow morning around half past nine, you can hear it and see what you think. Bring your tape recorder with you," he added. He heard no response. "You there, Elizabeth?" he said, his voice full of concern.

"OK, Joe," Elizabeth whispered in a hoarse voice. She was trying to understand and remember what Joe had just said. With effort, she cleared the mist in her mind.

"You OK, Elizabeth?" Joe asked again. "You sound a bit strange."

Somehow, she connected his words together and his message became clear.

"I'm OK, Joe. See you tomorrow." She hung up.

Joe heard the connection break; his eyebrows knitted. *What just happened?* This was not the same person he had met a couple of days ago. Something was seriously wrong.

Somehow, she had arrived at Joe's place of work and was shown upstairs by the receptionist. Joe was shocked. The woman who now stood in front of him was another person.

The cheerful, enthusiastic lady he had first met was gone. Her face was pale, her lips together with no trace of a smile. Half-closed, lifeless eyes. Her shoulders were slumped and everything about her drooped. Her simple "Hello Joe" was flat and emotionless. He had no idea how to react. The only thing he could do was to act normal, feeling very aware of Elizabeth now sitting slouched in the chair beside him.

"This is what I've got so far," Joe said as he switched on a large tape recorder. Elizabeth listened and Joe looked at her face. There was no reaction. The music had not touched her at all. She was staring down into her lap, playing with her fingers. She appeared to have no interest at all. Joe was uncomfortable and really wanted this to be over and Elizabeth gone.

"So, what do you think, Elizabeth?" he asked as politely as he could, holding back his irritation. After a moment she replied.

"It's a start, Joe," she said.

"OK, Elizabeth, but this is just the beginning. Now we're ready to start playing around with it," Joe replied. "As long as you're happy with the general idea and tempo, we can go further." Elizabeth nodded and muttered a few suggestions, which Joe noted down.

"OK," he said. "I will take these ideas to the musicians and let them play around with it for an hour or so. The inspiration always comes but only when it's good and ready."

"How long will it take to do that?" Elizabeth asked.

"About two hours," Joe replied.

"OK," said Elizabeth. "I will come back in a couple of hours." She got up, went back downstairs and left the building.

She was glad to be alone and wandered around the industrial area with aimless steps until it was time to return to the music company. Once again, she was back in Joe's domain.

157

"OK, Elizabeth," said Joe. "Try listening now with these headphones on." He passed them to her. She put them on and looked back down at her fingers. He pressed the buttons on the tape recorder and watched her face. For the first thirty seconds nothing changed. Elizabeth did not move. Then, all at once, she sat up straighter and her eyes flickered. Her mouth opened a fraction and a smile started to form. Pushing the headphones tighter to her ears, she began to move with the music. Joe was astounded with the sudden change and he found it frightening. She began to sway to the rhythm; colour returned to her cheeks and her eyes were now wide open. Joe let out a long, silent breath of relief. Elizabeth was emerging from the eerie mood she had been in and was returning to the person he had first met. He had now seen how fast Elizabeth's moods could change.

The sounds she heard bypassed her dark place. She heard only the notes, saw the instruments playing in her mind; the melody lifted her. "It's getting better, Joe," said Elizabeth, "but it still doesn't have that sparkle, that sharp individual hot spice that I'm looking for."

Her words heartened him. Her interest was back. She was involved again.

The phrase "individual hot spice" triggered Joe's imagination. With a quick "hang on a minute", he shot out of the door. He seemed to have been gone for ages and then he suddenly reappeared with a tape spool in his hand. He threaded the tape onto a tape recorder, and gave Elizabeth the headphones again. He sat down, took a deep breath, and pressed the "play" button.

The music reached her inner core and the peeled piece of the new picture returned to its place. The old painting was once again invisible, it's message no longer there. She got up and started moving in dancing steps, only held back by the cable of the headphones. The woman Joe had first met was back, and he looked relieved.

"Yes. Yes!" she cried; her eyes sparkling. "That's what I want. Now it is fantastic."

They talked rapidly about maybe changing a few other parts to just solos, and Joe jumped back into action.

"Now, I need to get busy," he said. "We have to break this tune down into the notes the individual instruments will play. What each of the kids will have to learn, and then I have to record all that onto your tape spools."

"Can I help you with any of that, Joe?" Elizabeth asked.

"Afraid not," Joe replied. He checked his watch.

"Don't work late for me, Joe," Elizabeth said. "You have worked more than enough already."

"It won't take that long as I'll get the musicians to help me," Joe replied. "If you give me your address, I can bring the tapes to you this evening when they're ready." Elizabeth gave Joe her address and said she looked forward to seeing him later.

She knew she had been close, and she was frightened. She had been that close before and had never understood how she had survived. She had to conquer the moods. She had to hold on to the light. She went into her bathroom and took out all the bottles of pills and threw them away. With a red lipstick, she drew a smiling face and a violin on the bathroom mirror. She went around her apartment and did the same on every mirror she had. She must be strong, she must be forgiving of herself and, maybe tonight, she would hold the sun in her hands.

Chapter 16

Flashing eyes, enraptured smiles, tongues longing to ask a hundred questions, lips licked with electrified anticipation, instantly replacing the looks of boredom, which had greeted Elizabeth on her arrival in the room with her tape recorder.

"OK, kids. I think we've had enough of just playing simple notes," she said. "Time to change gear; do what orchestras and bands do. You're going to make your first public performance."

Calling for hush as the children began cheering, Elizabeth waited for silence.

"It will mean hard work with lots of practice," continued Elizabeth. "It won't be easy, but I know you can do it."

"You mean play in front of people?" Grace shouted.

"That's the plan," Elizabeth replied.

The questions tumbled over each other in impatient excitement. "When?" "Where?" "What do we play?"

"Well," said Elizabeth, "first things first. I'm going to play you a piece of music I hope you will like, and hope you will all want to play. While you are listening to it, I'm going outside in the corridor, because I want you to be on your own when you hear it. Before I play it, I would like one of you to go and ask Miss Stratton, Mrs Hutchins and Miss Marigold, to come up here so they can hear it too."

Alexander rushed off and returned with the ladies a few minutes later.

Miss Stratton, with eyebrows fully arched in an astonished expression asked, "What's happening?" as she walked into the room.

"Sorry, Miss Stratton," Elizabeth answered. "I wanted this to be a surprise for everyone. Please gather round the table," she continued. "This tape recorder does not play very loudly, but I hope it will be enough for you to hear

160

the tune." She pressed the play button and then left the room.

Standing in the hall, head slightly bowed, eyes closed and her knuckles pressed to her mouth, Elizabeth waited. The waiting seemed to last for an eternity, and then the noise ignited. It was like a party with shouting, laughing, whooping and cheering. Opening the door, the children rushed towards her, grabbing her skirt; with Rachael grabbing her hand and pulling her into the room. The jabbering pandemonium was deafening.

Elizabeth held up her hand for them to quieten down and then asked, "Did you like it kids? Do you want to learn it and play it in public?" The answer was a very long and very loud, "Yeaaaaah."

If Elizabeth and the other grow-ups could have heard it, they would have heard a second, very loud conversation going on. The children heard, but they did not let on.

"Have you ever heard anything like that in your life?" exclaimed Veronica. "I mean, wow!"

"Wow, ain't even the start of it," cried Verity. "Wow does not cover it at all."

"You think you can do that solo without burnin' your wires out, Garry?" said Teddy with a laugh.

"Awesome, awesome," repeated Gilbert over and over, as if informing his acquaintances on the various planets he seemed to visit regularly.

"Unusual. Different, but amazingly good," drawled Charles.

"You won't be havin' any sinus trouble for a while, Camilla," quipped Dean.

"Don't be cheeky, Dean," retorted Camilla with a laugh. "It was nice to hear that your hides are gonna get a good beatin'." Caddie and Coral giggled.

The instruments prattled and cracked jokes, telling each

161

other that with such a piece, everything else would, well, be a bit boring.

Elizabeth felt the relief sweep over her. She couldn't speak. Hot tears of happiness stung her eyes. She had to sit down.

Miss Stratton and Mrs Hutchins came and sat next to her. "I'm not very musical as you know, Elizabeth," said Miss Stratton, "but that surely got my juices flowing."

"Haven't tap-danced like that in years," chipped in Mrs Hutchins. They looked across at Miss Marigold who was dancing around with the children, her faced flushed with exertion. Miss Stratton got up and asked for a little quiet.

"Well, children," began Miss Stratton, "I get the impression that you like Miss Elizabeth's idea?"

"It's great, Miss," Alexander cried out.

"We really, really want to do it," added Jasmine.

"It makes me very happy and very proud of you all to hear you say that," replied Miss Stratton with a big smile, "but," she continued, "you will all have to do exactly what Miss Elizabeth tells you to do if this is to be a success."

"We will," shouted Emily.

"Very well then," said Miss Stratton finally. "I will leave you with Miss Elizabeth to get things started." She and Mrs Hutchins left the room.

Miss Marigold stayed in the music room. "Before you start, Miss Rose," she said, "could you tell me if there is anything I can do to help with this, anything, anything at all? I really want to join in with it if there is something I can do." Elizabeth was overjoyed to hear Miss Marigold's offer.

"Oh, Miss Marigold," Elizabeth replied. "I was trying to find a way to ask you if you could do something, but I didn't want to burden you with even more work. If you're really sure, then there is something really important you can

162

help us with. I will explain it to you at the same time as I explain it to the children."

Elizabeth called the children to come to the table where the tape recorder was.

"OK, kids," she said. "You've all heard the piece as it is with everything together. To make it easier for you to learn, through the marvels of technology, I have been able to get the piece split into different parts." Elizabeth held up the other four reels of tape that Joe had made for her. "These tapes," continued Elizabeth, "have different parts and instruments on them. They are all labelled so you can see what instruments are on each tape. It will be easier for you to remember your tunes if they are not jumbled up all together as in the final piece. I will play the tapes with the different parts to each group three or four times, and when you tell me you have remembered enough, you can go to the other small rooms down the corridor and start practising. I have put a note on the doors telling you which rooms to use. Now," she continued, "as you know, I am not here on weekdays, unless I take holidays, and I can't take any more for a while, so Miss Marigold has kindly offered to help with this project. I will show her how to operate the tape recorder, so if you need to hear any of the parts again during the week, Miss Marigold will play the tape recorder for you. Is that OK with you, Miss Marigold?" asked Elizabeth, turning to her.

"Oh yes," replied Miss Marigold, with a broad, happy smile on her face. "I would love to do that."

"Very well," continued Elizabeth. "We only have about four weeks to learn this, so we start right now."

Elizabeth turned to the tape recorder and played the final piece again. Then she changed the tapes and played the separate parts each three times. "Do you think you can remember enough of the tunes to start practising now?" asked Elizabeth.

She never got a reply as the children were already scampering off to the their assigned rooms to practise. Only Emily and Harvey remained in the larger room as they would learn together. The drums were too bulky to be moved around.

Miss Marigold listened to what Elizabeth was telling her about the tape recorder. She thought everything was pretty simple and straightforward and asked if she could change a tape spool to make sure she had understood the process correctly. This she did with ease and then Elizabeth gave her the instruction book in case anything "funny" happened. She heard Harvey practising the clarinet and Emily banging out her drum rolls. Saying good bye to Miss Marigold, Elizabeth went out into the corridor and smiled as she heard the other instruments playing. The notes she heard were clear and sharp, and she was thrilled. She went down to Miss Stratton's sitting room where she found her and Mrs Hutchins chatting.

"I'm going to go home now," she said. "I feel quite exhausted."

"Do you think they can do it?" asked Miss Stratton.

"Oh, I know they can," Elizabeth replied. "I know they can."

Chapter 17

"Is it always like this when children learn to play?" she asked.

"No, it isn't, Miss Marigold," replied Elizabeth in a whisper. "I don't understand how they do it either, but I have accepted that they can and I leave it at that."

"Mmm," replied Miss Marigold, "it's so exciting though, isn't it? Oh, just one other thing, Miss Rose," she continued. "I'm maybe being silly, but with the guitars, they don't seem to sound the same as the guitars on the tape. There seems to be something missing somehow."

"How do you mean? Miss Marigold," asked Elizabeth, immediately worried.

"Well," said Miss Marigold, "it's as if it's missing a bit of body, a bit of volume, there's a lack of some sort of…" she paused searching for a word, "…denseness, I suppose you could call it. Our guitars sound a bit tinny."

Elizabeth was puzzled and then her hand shot to her mouth. "You're right, Miss Marigold," she cried, as she realised that the electric guitars were playing without amplifiers. She had forgotten all about these extra needs, and a slight panic struck her. *What am I going to do?* There's nothing I can do right now, she rapidly concluded, but she would have to get something sorted out before the performance. She went to the room where Brandon and Max were practising and heard for herself that the sound was without doubt "tinny". She then went round and listened to each section and showered praise and encouragement on all the children.

"It's just like old times," murmured Celia in her soft, happy voice to Faith. "Just like getting ready for a big concert again. I can hardly believe it."

In another room, Gilbert was saying to Max that he

hoped there wouldn't be a guy in a fancy suit waving a white stick at them when they were playin'. "Too much authority, man, too much authority, can't handle all of that. Got to go with the beat and the soul," he ended, before he went off to converse with his friends in another world.

"Joe," said Elizabeth, with the slight panic still in her voice when she called him on Monday. "I have a little problem," she rushed on. "I need two amplifiers for the guitars and I have no idea where to get them."

"Is that all?" replied Joe, with a laugh. "That's no problem at all. How big you want 'em? Where are you playin'?"

Elizabeth told him where they were going to perform.

"OK," replied Joe. "I can get a couple of amps to suit that. Where do you want me to bring them and when?"

Elizabeth asked him if he could bring them to Saint Etheldreda's next Saturday afternoon and then asked, "Are they heavy, Joe?" as she had no idea.

"No, they're not too bad," replied Joe. "I can carry one on my own if I have to, but it's pretty easy with two."

Full of relief, Elizabeth gave Joe the address of the Foundation and said she looked forward to seeing him on Saturday. She thanked him for his help.

Joe replied, "You're welcome."

As he had promised, five days later Joe arrived at the Foundation. Elizabeth had been watching from a second-floor window and when she saw a small, white van pull up outside the building, she called Brandon and Max to come quickly with her. They hurried down the stairs to the front door and went down the steps to see Joe getting out.

"Hi, Elizabeth," said Joe. "I've got the amps in the back. I've also brought some extension cables in case you need them."

Elizabeth introduced Joe to Brandon and Max and told him these were the two boys who were playing the guitars.

"Don't blow your ears off with these babies," said Joe with a laugh. "They got some power."

"Is it OK just to plug them into normal sockets?" asked Elizabeth.

"It's OK," replied Joe, "so long as you don't turn them up more than half way. More than that, you may blow fuses, depending on how much current your sockets can take."

Elizabeth told Brandon and Max that this was the gentleman who had made it all possible by creating the music in the first place. The boys were awestruck. When the amplifiers and cables had been taken out of the van, Joe had driven off after saying "bye" to Elizabeth. He had a feeling of great satisfaction, pride, achievement, and that he had actually done something quite special.

They took the amplifiers upstairs and plugged them into two separate sockets hoping that the building's electrical system could cope. Next, they connected the guitars to the amplifiers and Elizabeth checked that the volume was set at around a quarter.

"We're back in business, man," said Gilbert to Gary, almost drooling with anticipation. "I feel all together again man, you know, sort of whole again."

"OK, you two," Elizabeth said to Brandon and Max in their practising room. "Give it a go."

The pounding steps hammering up the stairs accompanied by screams of "Stop! For glory's sake, stop," announcing the arrival of Miss Stratton and Mrs Hutchins. The moment Brandon's fingers had strummed his guitar, they had shot out of their chairs as if they had just been fired out of ejector seats.

"What are you trying to do, blow all the windows out?"

167

cried Miss Stratton, trying to catch her breath from her run – the fastest she had run for years. She grabbed the back of a chair to steady herself and wheezed like an old boiler. Elizabeth, who had leapt to the amplifiers to turn them down when Brandon had started playing, apologised to Miss Stratton and Mrs Hutchins for the loud noise and for startling them. The other children had also shot out into the corridor and crowded around the door to the room where Brandon and Max were playing to see what was going on.

Miss Stratton, who had calmed down a bit, replied, "Oh, it's OK, my dear. It just startled us both a bit, that's all, but if you could make sure we've still got windows and doors at the end of today, I would very much appreciate it," she ended, with a big laugh.

After Miss Stratton and Mrs Hutchins had returned to their sitting room, the children went back to practising. Miss Marigold was constantly on the move, going from room to room asking if each group wanted to hear more of their notes or if they wanted to hear something again. She was glad she was wearing her slippers. When Elizabeth asked her if everything was going OK, Miss Marigold replied with a laugh, "The only sore point is the tip of my finger."

Elizabeth was thrilled with the progress the children were making. Sure, various parts still needed more practice; she pointed these out to the children concerned. The whole thing could go a lot smoother, but it was all coming along better than she had hoped.

The month of the summer solstice was coming to an end. The time had come for a complete dress rehearsal and the children were all together in the large room and had made themselves comfortable.

"OK, kids," said Elizabeth. "If you're all ready, we will

start." The children nodded and raised their instruments to play. Emily picked up her drumsticks and the music began.

Elizabeth was entranced. It took her a few seconds to realise the children had stopped playing. She started to clap and then, throwing her arms wide open, she indicated that she wanted to hug them all. She had no words that would adequately portray her pride in what these children had achieved; she felt the small tears of joy trickle down her cheeks.

Once more composed, she asked them to play it again, this time when Miss Stratton, Mrs Hutchins and Miss Marigold were in attendance. Afterwards, all the ladies agreed that this was truly remarkable. The individual pieces of the music puzzle were almost perfect, but the seams where they joined needed to be smoothed and polished. They needed more practice for them to slot invisibly together.

"OK, kids," said Elizabeth. "I will come here on Friday after I have finished at my work. You will be here all that day, as the school holidays will have started. Spend those days practising until you are really happy with everything and to make sure you are all playing together. Now, one more important thing needs to be done." Elizabeth continued, "and that is to choose a name. Whether you are an orchestra or a band, I don't know. I will leave that for you to decide. So, if over the next couple of days, you can think of a name, please let Miss Stratton know by Tuesday if you can." Elizabeth went over to Dean's big bass drum and looked at it, roughly noting the size of it, and how it was made. She then returned to the door to go down to the kitchen to have a cup of tea.

As she was going out of the room, Zac asked Elizabeth where they were actually going to play. The children waited inquisitively for the answer.

After checking with the city authorities, Elizabeth had

planned the performance on the wide pavement outside the Foundation. It was the only place they could do it because the park had no electricity supply and they did not have the money to rent a hall. She did not want to tell the children this, as she wanted it to be a surprise.

"Never mind that for the moment," answered Elizabeth with a smile. "You just concentrate on getting everything right. I will tell you where you are going to play when we get nearer the time."

"Will there be lots of people there?" asked Faith.

"I really don't know the answer to that, Faith," Elizabeth replied. "We will just have to wait and see how many people turn up." Elizabeth turned and left the music room with a parting comment of "Keep up the good work, kids. This is going to be great. See you all next Friday."

Elizabeth had her usual cup of tea with Miss Stratton and Mrs Hutchins. Miss Marigold had said she would stay with the children in case they needed her. Elizabeth informed Miss Stratton about her request for the children to come up with a name, and that she would call her on Tuesday evening, if that was OK, to find out what the children wanted to call themselves. Elizabeth explained what she intended to do with that information. She also suggested that it might be nice to contact the people who had become involved with the children to let them know about the performance in case they wanted to come. Miss Stratton agreed that it would be a very nice gesture.

"Sorry to trouble you, Miss," Brandon said, "but Miss Elizabeth asked us to think of a name for our band, so we have chosen the name we would like. Miss Elizabeth said to tell Miss Stratton, so we've written the name down on this piece of paper. Could you give it to Miss Stratton for us, please?"

"Certainly, Brandon," replied Miss Marigold. Brandon handed the folded piece of paper to Miss Marigold before walking away. Miss Marigold closed the sitting-room door and went over to Miss Stratton. "The children have decided on a name for their band." She handed the piece of paper to Miss Stratton. Miss Stratton took the paper, opened it and looked at the name.

"Oh," she cried. "That won't do at all. Look what they have written, Mrs Hutchins." She passed the piece of paper to her. Miss Hutchins looked at the name the children had written.

"What's wrong with that?" asked Mrs Hutchins. "I think that's a great name. It's old and new combined, sort of catchy," she concluded.

"But look at the spelling," said Miss Stratton. "I don't want people to think we are illiterate. The word 'Rocking' has a 'G' at the end of it not an 'N'." Without realising she had said it, Mrs Hutchins replied with a laugh, "Oh, don't be such a stick-in-the-mud, Abby."

Miss Stratton looked startled and surprised for a moment, and then a warm smile came over her face. "Thank you for saying that," she whispered. "It's been a long time."

Mrs Hutchins looked a bit confused. "How do you mean, Miss Stratton?" she asked.

"You called me by my first name," replied Miss Stratton. "It has suddenly made me realise that we three have also become a family, like three big sisters looking after a large family of much younger children. This place has become home to all of us too."

Without having to say anything, the three ladies got up and hugged each other. Abigail Stratton, Jennifer Hutchins and Susanna Marigold stood still for a few moments in a loving, comfortable, belonging silence.

They broke away, and Abigail Stratton took the paper with the name the children had written, went to the table and picked up a pen. With a flourish, she added the apostrophe after the letter "N" and said, "OK, I can live with that."

Going briefly to her room, Abigail Stratton came back and asked Jennifer and Susanna a quick question. She then opened her bottle of sherry.

Elizabeth called the Foundation and Miss Marigold answered.

"Could I speak to Miss Stratton please?" she asked.

"I'm sorry, Miss Rose, but she is not back from her meeting at the Juvenile Support office yet," Miss Marigold said. "Can I help you with anything?"

Elizabeth explained she was calling to ask if the children had come up with a name yet.

"Oh, I know about that," said Miss Marigold. "Miss Stratton told me about it and said I should tell you if she was delayed at her meeting." Miss Marigold told Elizabeth the story of the name, and Miss Stratton's reaction to the missing apostrophe. Elizabeth burst out laughing and Miss Marigold was taken with a fit of giggles.

During her lunch break the next day, Elizabeth went to the Music Shop. As she went in, the manager saw her and he went over and greeted her.

"How are you, Miss Rose?" he said with a genuine smile. "I hope you are well, and how is the project with your children coming along?"

Elizabeth returned the greeting and told him the project was going fine.

"Actually," continued Elizabeth, "that's the reason I'm here." She explained to the manager what she wanted and he replied that it was no problem as the Music Shop had a good working relationship with another company close by that could produce what Elizabeth required.

"Does it take long," enquired Elizabeth, "as I'm afraid I have left it a bit late?"

"They can make these things very fast, Miss Rose," the manager replied. "It can be ready to pick up from here by Friday morning, if that is acceptable."

"That's perfect," replied Elizabeth with relief. She then continued to tell him about the performance they had planned for the coming Saturday and told him that she hoped he would be able to come and see it.

"I would be delighted," the manager replied.

The Hawk had also been very busy. First, his meeting with Mr Robson at the Juvenile Support Department had gone well. Then he had spent quite a lot of time arranging for the purchase and delivery of various items he wanted and for a local contractor to carry out some work for him. He had also taken his ex-clerk, Mr Francis, out to lunch, as without his assistance and local knowledge, the Hawk would not have been able to complete what he wanted to do. Now, as the weekend approached, he sat in his apartment feeling very content. He was very much looking forward to the coming days.

The cardboard tube was in her hand. The final touch she had collected from the Music Shop that Friday morning. Kneeling in front of the big white face of Dean, the bass drum, Elizabeth removed the top of the tube and very slowly slid out the roll of thin white paper material. Taking the small red tab at the edge of the roll, she placed it where the manager at the Music Shop had told her. Then, carefully but firmly pressing the thin paper against the drum skin, she let the paper unroll until it covered the entire face of the drum. She smoothed her hand over the paper with gentle pressure, and after making sure that the paper was firmly stuck to the drum, she took the small tab between her fingers and pulled downwards. The white covering peeled

173

away, leaving the letters stuck to the surface. In an arc around the top and bottom of the drum skin, in gold letters edged with green, and a single word in bright red, written at a slant in a modern flowing style across the middle, Dean's bass drum told the world in pride and beauty, that this was:

Saint Etheldreda's *Rockin'* Orchestra

The children were thrilled.

"OK kids," she said, "just for me. Play the music again so I can stop these butterflies in my tummy. I know you can do it, but I need to check that everything is together."

The children did as she asked and Elizabeth was satisfied. They were ready.

Looking out of the window, she saw it was a bright, sunny afternoon. "Why don't you go out for a walk?" she said. "Get some fresh air inside you, if that's OK with you, Miss Marigold?" added Elizabeth, turning to her. Miss Marigold nodded and said that she thought that was a very good idea.

"Don't worry about tomorrow. It will be fine. It will be fun," said Elizabeth, and the children scurried out of the music room.

Elizabeth and Miss Marigold went down to the kitchen and found Miss Stratton and Mrs Hutchins sitting at the kitchen table chatting. They looked up when Elizabeth and Miss Marigold came in.

"All set for tomorrow?" asked Miss Stratton.

"All set, Miss Stratton," Elizabeth replied.

"The children have gone out to the park to get some fresh air, Abby," said Miss Marigold.

"That's fine, Susanna," replied Abigail.

Elizabeth looked startled for a moment. It was the first time she had heard them call each other by their first names. Abigail noticed. "Please sit down, my dear," she said to Elizabeth. "We have all known each other for some little time now," said Abigail Stratton, in a gentle voice. "We have grown into a family, so now we want to be like a family. We three," she continued, her hand sweeping round to include Jennifer Hutchins, Susanna Marigold and herself, "we're like sisters now, and as far as we are concerned, you are part of our family too, Elizabeth."

Elizabeth felt the tears in her eyes. She dared not speak in case they overflowed and ran down her cheeks. Abigail Stratton put her hand over Elizabeth's and said in a soft, embracing voice, "Welcome."

Elizabeth woke early, adrenalin flooding into every part of her. Throwing open the curtains, she glanced up at the cloudless sky, the sun's blazing light filling the summer's day with glory. Dressing and preparing herself for the day, she forced herself to eat a piece of toast to quell the nervous flutters in her stomach and drank a cup of coffee. It was still early, and the buses would not have started to operate. Knowing that Saint Etheldreda's was about an hour walk away, she took her handbag, left her apartment, and was soon walking at a steady pace along residential streets and passing clusters of corner shops until she reached the road which ran in front of the Foundation. She continued along the road and then, in the distance, she noticed something unusual. Her eyes narrowed and her pace quickened; a feeling of worry, bordering on slight panic, started aching within her, making her stomach flutter again. She got closer and her pace increased so that now she was running. Her heart was thumping, her mouth open, breathing in rapid gasps; the feeling that was now definitely panic, rising and rising, before she reached the point of all her focus. She stopped and put a hand against the wall to steady herself. *It could not be happening. It could not be true.* A great wailing cry burst from her trembling lips, and she raised her arms above her head with fists clenched tight as if to beat off an attacker. There in an arc on the wide pavement where she had hoped to realise so many dreams for herself, the children and all at Saint Etheldreda's, two men leant on their shovels in a casual pose. The two piles of paving stones and three mounds of earth all stood guard over a big hole in the ground.

Chapter 18

"OK," cried out Emily, "on four. One, two, three, four," and with the thunder of a drum roll, followed by a great crash on the cymbal, the heavy thump of the bass drum giving the beat, Saint Etheldreda's Rockin' Orchestra began their debut performance with a very modern, unique and inspiring version of the *Prelude to the Holberg Suite*.

The cry had stopped with a sharp snap of her jaw. The image of the smiling face and violin on her bathroom mirror flashed before her, and instead of sinking into despair, her anguish turned to rage. She would not let the black moods win. Flying up the steps, she jammed her finger hard on the doorbell and kept pushing; the bell continuously ringing.

The running footsteps behind the door stopped, the key turned in the lock and the door was flung open with force. A very annoyed and irate Miss Stratton stood panting in the doorway. Her acute displeasure evaporated in an instant and was replaced with a look of shocked concern when she saw Elizabeth, with a face full of fury, standing before her.

"Whatever's the matter, Elizabeth?" she cried.

Five seconds later she was standing by the large hole in the ground, demanding answers from the workmen. On hearing their casual replies, Miss Stratton snapped, "We'll see about that!" She then charged back up the steps to her office, wrenched the telephone receiver from its cradle and dialled a private number; the home of Mr Robson from the Juvenile Support Department. The call set in motion a series of other telephone calls that bounced forwards like a flat stone skimming across the surface of a pond until it had reached the ear of the man responsible to the city for outside and underground electrical repairs and maintenance. One hour later, a van screeched to a halt outside the Foundation and three men leapt out. One of them could have been, in a possible previous life, a slave driver. Within two hours, the work that the first workmen had planned to spin out for an entire day, in order to earn a nice sum of overtime, had been completed. The underground electrical fault had been repaired and tested. The workmen had crawled wearily to their van, limping with exhaustion. With sweat pouring off them, they had got into the vehicle and driven away. The slave driver and his two companions had followed. No trace of their work remained to be seen.

During this episode, Brandon had been with the other children back to the park. Miss Marigold had suggested this little excursion in order to try and help them control their nerves and get some fresh air. They had noticed the hole in the pavement, but not yet knowing where they were going to perform, they gave it scant attention. On their return, the reinstalled pavement did not register with them as their focus and jittery nerves were completely concentrated on what they were about to do.

Elizabeth stood looking at the children who were arranged in a semi-circle on the wide pavement trying not to cry. Next to her stood Abigail Stratton, Susanna Marigold, Jennifer Hutchins and a tall, slim gentleman with swept-back silver hair that she did not know. For the next four minutes she was rigid, the perfect, faultless music surrounding her in a cocoon. And then the music stopped. A huge cheer erupted, hands were clapping and quickly turning around, she saw Mario, Maria, Alfredo, Ricardo and Stephano; the manager of the Music Shop, Joe, and other people whom she didn't know, talking to Miss Stratton. The sound of horns honking drew her attention to the street, and she saw that cars had stopped, the drivers, having got out of their vehicles, were clapping. Some were shouting, "Play it again, kids. Play it again."

Elizabeth turned back to the children. Their faces were radiant. Emily was looking back at her, brows furrowed upwards as if asking a question. Elizabeth nodded.

Emily's clear voice rang out again. "One, two, three, four." as Saint Etheldreda's Rockin' Orchestra launched into their first encore.

The telephones were starting to ring almost continuously. A rather harassed officer knocked on the glass-panelled door where he could see a large, red-faced man, who obviously liked his food, sitting at his desk with his uniform jacket unbuttoned. He looked up as the door opened and the officer came in.

"Yeah?" he asked.

"Seems a bit of a problem is occurrin' chief," said the officer.

"What sort of problem?" said the chief, instantly attentive.

"Well, according to a lot of folks callin' in, and also from our guys out on the street callin' in over their car radios, seems somethin's happenin' over the park end of the city." The officer gave the name of the street.

"The guys are askin' if you wouldn't mind goin' over there to sort somethin' out 'cause they're strugglin'," the officer concluded.

The chief thought for a moment and then stood up. He buttoned up his uniform jacket and told the officer to get his car around to the front.

"Yes, chief," answered the officer, and with rapid steps he left the room.

"All I needed on a Saturday," grumbled the chief to himself as he strode out of his office. He went down the stairs, walked out of the building, and heaved himself into the front seat of the patrol car next to the driver. He told the driver the name of the street he wanted to go to, and with blue lights flashing and the siren going, the officer in charge of the city's traffic roared out of the police station yard with tyres smoking.

They hit the gridlocked traffic some distance away from where the traffic chief wanted to be. He had no choice. He had to get out of the patrol car and walk. His temper was rising fast, and by the time he was approaching Saint Etheldreda's Foundation, after struggling to make his way through crowds of people all clapping and swaying to the music, which he now heard loud and clear, his face was a dark shade of purple. With sweat pouring off him, he arrived at the centre of where the action was taking place, and he barked out in a rather wheezy voice, "Who's in charge here? I wanna see the person in charge."

Miss Stratton, who had been expecting some sort of official visit as soon as she had seen all the cars stopped in the road, and the amount of people who had gathered in the street, extended her hand, and, with a dazzling smile and smooth voice said, "That would be me, officer. Please do come in."

With a grunt, the traffic chief followed Miss Stratton into Saint Etheldreda's and she took him into the kitchen. Organised as ever, Miss Stratton had put Mrs Hutchins on standby as soon as she saw the situation outside developing. She asked the traffic chief if he would like tea or coffee.

"Tell me what's happenin' first ma'am," said the traffic chief, trying to be as polite as he could, even though he felt like shouting his head off, as he would if addressing a bunch of new recruits.

"Let me explain," said Miss Stratton, "but first, please, do sit down officer, and have something to drink. You look a bit exhausted."

The traffic chief realised that he really needed to sit

down, so he sank with gratitude into the chair that Miss Stratton had indicated. "Coffee would be fine," he said in a voice that began to sound a little more human. "Thank you, ma'am," he added, shortly after.

Mrs Hutchins had, in the meantime, gone to her larder and taken out the large Victoria sponge cake, which she had made for later, and placed it on the table. She turned to her coffee peculator, poured out a large cup of coffee, and placed it on the table in front of the traffic chief, together with a bowl of sugar lumps and a small jug of cream.

"Would you like a slice of cake, officer?" Mrs Hutchins asked.

The traffic chief, who had a very sweet tooth, looked at the cake and replied, "Well, that would be very nice, ma'am."

Miss Stratton began her explanation of what was happening outside, and she also included a short history of Saint Etheldreda's Foundation, what the Foundation did, and why she had thirteen children sitting outside playing music.

As Miss Stratton's explanation unfolded, the traffic chief's thoughts had begun to drift away and were concentrating themselves on Mrs Hutchins's Victoria sponge cake. He had eaten plenty of cake in his time, as the size of his waistband showed, but this, well, this was something else. It must be without doubt the most delicious Victoria sponge he had ever tasted. Suddenly returning his mind to the reason he was there, he heard Miss Stratton saying, "Well, that's all there is to say, officer."

Having missed a good part of what Miss Stratton had actually said, due to his preoccupation with the sponge cake, the chief of the city's traffic department was stuck for a reply. "Well ma'am," he said, thinking very quickly, "if that's how it is, then OK. Just stop the kids playin' and then I can try to sort out the mess out there." He got up, feeling that his waistband was even tighter than usual, and said, "Please get your kids to stop now ma'am, otherwise I'll have a whole load of explainin' to do."

As he was leaving the kitchen, Mrs Hutchins asked, "Would you like to take the rest of this cake with you, officer? You seemed to enjoy it so much. Here, let me put it in a bag for you." Mrs Hutchins wrapped the remaining cake into a thick wad of kitchen tissue paper and put it into a large paper bag. She handed the bag to the traffic chief, who accepted it rather shyly, saying, "Well, that's mighty kind and generous of you, ma'am."

Miss Stratton escorted the traffic chief to the front door, which was still open, and out to the top of the steps. She went quickly to Elizabeth and whispered to her, to which Elizabeth nodded. Returning to the traffic chief, Miss Stratton said that the children would stop playing in a couple of minutes after they had finished what was now their ninth encore, and the traffic chief replied, "Thank you, ma'am."

As the crowds of people roared and clapped, Elizabeth went and stood in front of the children with tears of pure joy streaming down her cheeks. Finally, she brought herself under control, but with her voice still a bit unsteady, she said, "That was truly amazing, kids. I'm so, so proud of you."

She told them that it was time to stop now, and with great smiles of pride and achievement on their faces, they started to take the chairs and instruments back inside. Elizabeth joined the other ladies at the top of the steps and they all hugged each other. They stood and looked at the crowds in the street and saw the traffic chief waving his arms about like a crazy windmill, still clutching his bag with the Victoria sponge cake.

"Oh, look what he's doing with that poor cake," cried Mrs Hutchins. She paused and then added, "I hope he likes crumbs."

Like four very young, carefree girls, Abigail Stratton, Susanne Marigold, Jennifer Hutchins and Elizabeth Rose burst into an uncontrollable fit of giggles.

Chapter 19

The room that had been fizzing and crackling with exploding emotions slowly became hushed, calm, an oasis of utter contentment. The shrieks, clapping, hugging and triumphant laughter gave way to smiles and flashing eyes blazing out happiness, fulfilment and joy. Miss Stratton now stood in front of the children with Miss Marigold, Mrs Hutchins and Elizabeth beside her.

"So, once again everyone, we, and she indicated with her outstretched hand Miss Marigold, Mrs Hutchins and Elizabeth, we are all so very proud of you for what you have achieved today. You have all been truly amazing."

"We couldn't have done it without all of you," said Faith. "You let us have the instruments and got them fixed, Miss Marigold helped us so much with learning the tune, Mrs Hutchins always kept us going with kind words and encouragement and Miss Elizabeth..." She stopped and clenched her teeth to control her emotions. "Miss Elizabeth," Faith continued, "you are just the best."

"You're better than the best, Miss Elizabeth," shouted Grace.

"As you say Faith and Grace, we owe so much to Miss Elizabeth and everything she has done here," Miss Stratton replied.

Elizabeth had been standing with her head bowed. How could a person change so much in just a few hours? She felt renewed, reborn and a wonderful feeling of self- confidence she had never had before. She knew she was now able to control the terrible mood swings, to take charge of her life and not let uncontrollable emotions dictate her every thought. She had an inner glow with a sense of belonging, a purpose in life and hope. A picture in her mind of these children playing beautiful music on the street was a key which unlocked the chains of misery which had bound her for so long. The painful memories of the times her life had nearly ended, and the desolation of carrying on when somehow she had kept living, seemed to be from the mind of another person. She now had strength to be pro-active instead of always being re-active, and all of this was due to feeling useful, feeling wanted and being part of helping these children achieve something wonderful. She now looked up and smiled. "I should be thanking all of you," she said. She looked at the children and then back at Miss Stratton, Miss Marigold and Mrs Hutchins. "Thank you for welcoming me to your family and all you have done for me. Coming back to this place and meeting all of you means so much to me."

"I don't want today to end," said Jasmine. "I want it to go on for ever!"

"That's a lovely thought, Jasmine and today is not over yet," Miss Stratton said. "We are going to have a celebration party with all sorts of delicious cakes and jellies that Mrs Hutchins has prepared for us. How long do you need to get everything ready, Jennifer?"

"Oh, about an hour," Mrs Hutchins replied.

"I'll give you a hand, Jennifer," said Miss Marigold. "I really feel that I need to be busy."

"Oh, thanks Susanna," Mrs Hutchins replied. "That would be a great help."

"OK then," said Miss Stratton. "I think it's time you cleaned your instruments and put them safely away. Miss Elizabeth and I are going down to our sitting room. Please come down to the kitchen in about an hour." The adults left the room.

"Well," said Charles, drawing out the word in his slow cultural drawl. "I think the old saying of 'you cannot teach a dog new tricks' should definitely be thrown in the dustbin. Today was wonderfully astounding."

"You can say that again, Charlie; sorry, I mean, Charles. I haven't felt so young in years," said Verity. "What a rhythm! What a sound! All those people shouting and clapping on the street. It was fantastic."

Charles looked at Harvey. "By the way, Harvey," he said, "you played me beautifully. You have remarkable fingers, strong yet sensitive."

"He gets that from picking locks," said Evie.

"Really," Charles replied. "You must tell me about that sometime, Harvey."

Harvey swelled with pride.

"Maybe this is that new sound you mentioned a while ago, Gilbert," continued Charles. "Something about Mozart, Bach, dogs and teeth."

Gilbert looked a bit confused and then his eyes brightened. "Oh yeah, yeah, 'Mozibark' man," he said. The old stuff with a new bite. Yeah, yeah. Could be big, man. 'Mozibark' music. A brand-new sound."

"Just goes to show," said Dean. "It is possible to combine the old and the new and create something really inspiring."

"So," said Veronica. "Now we are a proper orchestral family. A family of musicians, all ready to have fun and play great music. I hope it will happen that we play often, but I think there is something you kids need to do first. It would be great if you learnt to read music. That way, things will go much easier. Maybe you could ask your lovely Miss Elizabeth to teach you?"

"That's a great idea, Veronica," said Rachael. "We will ask her if she will teach us."

"You talk about families, Veronica," said Faith. "I don't know exactly how everyone else feels, but because we have done all this together, it makes me feel like we really are a family now. I feel I'm with my brothers and sisters and this is our home. Miss Stratton, Miss Marigold Mrs Hutchins and Miss Elizabeth are like the parents most of us never knew."

Rachael quickly looked at Emily and saw the quiver of her lips. She went and put her arm around the young girl's shoulders. "Without you, Emily, we would never have played the wonderful music today. Because your mummy and daddy loved music so much, you remembered that tune you used to drive us crazy with. That led to us meeting Miss Elizabeth. I know you will always miss them, but maybe it is because of them that today happened. Maybe there is a heaven, and they are there smiling down on you, doing everything they can to make you happy again. Maybe it is because of them that we can hear and speak to Veronica, Dean, Charles, Teddy, Celia and all the other instruments. Maybe this is what they want for you, to make you happy through the music they loved so much."

"What a beautiful thought," said Camilla.

"I know that's a lot of maybes," Rachael continued, "but it would explain so much about what has happened to us."

"Maybe even Saint Ettie herself was helping," said Evie.

Emily looked up at Rachael. "Do you really think that they are in heaven and doing all this for me, doing all this for us?"

"It could be that Rachael is right. I knew you were special, Emily, from the first moment we met," said Dean.

"It is hard not to be sad and I miss my mummy and daddy so much," said Emily. "But like you say, I feel really close to all of you and would love to be your sister. The music does help to make me feel better."

"Let the music lift your spirits, Emily, especially when

187

you feel sadness," said Celia. "That is the wonder of it. It can heal so much."

Emily let out a long sigh. "Thanks everyone. I will try to remember what you have said. By the way Camilla, I hope I didn't hurt you too much when I hit you hard with the drumsticks."

"The harder the better," Camilla replied. "That way I can really make a great sound and a good bang does wonders for my sinuses."

The mood in the room instantly lightened, and laughter returned.

"I think it's time for you kids to get ready for your party," said Violet after a few minutes of loud laughing and giggling.

"I'll go with that," said Veronica. "So, kids, clean us up, put us safe and snug, and then have a great celebration party."

They had gorged themselves on jellies, cakes and ice-cream and now sat full and contented around the kitchen table. "We have been talking," began Brandon, aiming his conversation at Miss Stratton and Elizabeth. "We would really love to play more music like today, either outside or somewhere else. Do you think we could do that?"

"Well," Miss Stratton replied. "That depends on Miss Elizabeth." She turned to Elizabeth with an enquiring expression on her face.

"Oh, I would love to if you are OK with it, Abigail," said Elizabeth.

"Fine by me," replied Miss Stratton.

"Another thing, please Miss Elizabeth," said Rachael. "Could you teach us how to read music? Maybe it would make learning new tunes a lot easier."

"Sure," Elizabeth replied. "It would be a lot easier for

me to do that if I had a piano, but I'm sure we can find a way around that."

"Maybe we can talk about that next week, Elizabeth," said Miss Stratton. "I'm sure we can work something out." She looked back at the children. "Miss Elizabeth, Miss Marigold and I have been talking too," she continued, "and considering what you have just asked about playing again, I think Miss Elizabeth has something to say to you."

"I'm not sure if this is right," Elizabeth began, "but Miss Stratton thinks that the instruments still belong to me. After everything you have achieved and the fantastic day we have had today, then I want to give these instruments to each of you. If you want to, you can keep the instrument that you play. I hope they will bring you much happiness and joy."

"You really mean that we can always keep them?" asked Jasmine loudly. "That they are ours now forever?"

"Yes," Elizabeth replied. "That's exactly what I mean." There were loud gasps and faces filled with wide eyes, open mouths and expressions of starling surprise.

"This is probably the best present I have ever had," said Freya. "Thank you so much, Miss Elizabeth. It's really kind of you."

"You are all very welcome," Elizabeth replied.

"We all feel like we are brothers and sisters now, that this is our real home," said Faith.

It lasted but a second, but during that second, a thousand memories surged through the minds of four adults remembering both good times and bad. But for each of them, Faith's words triggered an immense, overwhelming feeling of accomplishment, that they had been able to create a loving family and bring so much happiness to these children.

"Your words touch me more than you can ever imagine," Miss Stratton said.

"You may not know this, kids," said Susanne Marigold, "but like you, I was brought up in an orphanage. I never knew my real mummy or daddy. So, I know just how you're feeling right now because, since I have been here at Saint Etheldreda's, I feel the same way. To know that others love you and care about you is so wonderful, and having found this family, I never want to lose it. When the time comes and each of you leave Saint Etheldreda's and go out into the world, please, always stay in touch and keep this family alive. Families are there for each other even if they live far apart."

"Talking of new beginnings," said Jennifer Hutchins with a huge grin on her face, "I think once a week everybody in this family, and I mean everybody, should roll up their sleeves and help with the washing up! You don't think I'm going to clean up all this on my own, do you?"

The room erupted with spontaneous laughter. "OK, Mrs Hutchins," said Brendon. "We will show you all how it's done."

"Cheek," laughed Miss Stratton as she rolled up the sleeves of her cardigan.

With all the washing up completed, Elizabeth glanced at her watch. "So, everyone, I really do not want today to end, but I have to get going as I need to get a few things in the city before the shops close. Hopefully, I will see you all next week."

Everyone went with Elizabeth to the front door and after saying, smiling, hugging and waving goodbyes, she left the Foundation and made her way to the shopping centre.

After Elizabeth had left, Miss Stratton asked everyone to go back to the kitchen and there she explained some of what she had planned for the next day.

Chapter 20

The Hawk finished reading the page and put the newspaper down on his table. He looked again at the bold headline and the picture:

GRIDLOCK AT SAINT ETHELDREDA'S FOUNDATION

He smiled. The picture had captured perfectly the image he had seen for himself the day before. He would contact the newspaper and try to obtain a copy of it. Getting up from his chair, he got himself ready to go out.

Elizabeth, sipping a cup of coffee, had never felt such happiness or sense of achievement in her life before. Her phone rang and she picked it up.

"Elizabeth," said Abigail Stratton. "Good morning, how are you? Did you sleep well?"

"Like in paradise, thank you, Abigail," Elizabeth replied.

"Well," continued Abigail, "I'm sorry if this is all a bit at short notice, but all of us here would love it if you could come and have lunch with us today?"

"I would love to," Elizabeth replied before quickly glancing at her clock. "I'm not sure just when I can get there. I will have to check the bus times."

"Nonsense," replied Abigail emphatically. "A taxi will be outside your apartment in an hour."

Elizabeth arrived at the Foundation and was greeted by Susanna Marigold. They went into the kitchen where everyone else had gathered; they all clapped when she entered. The children ran towards her and wrapped their arms around her, and she ruffled the hair of those closest to her.

"It's eleven o'clock Elizabeth, and we usually eat at around twelve." Miss Stratton said. "There are a couple of things I would like to speak to you about for five minutes, and then we will go for a quick walk to the park and leave Mrs Hutchins in peace."

Elizabeth joined Abigail in her office.

"Well," Abigail began. "The little tape recorder that you have here, if you agree, we would like to buy it from you. We can put it to various uses, but if you would prefer to keep it, that is also fine."

Elizabeth thought for a moment and then replied, "I don't really need it for anything now, so if you want it that's fine."

"Good," said Abigail and opened her desk draw. She gave Elizabeth one of the cheques the Hawk had given her.

"Oh, Abigail," cried Elizabeth. "This is too much. This is the price I paid for it new."

"Please don't quibble, Elizabeth," said Abigail Stratton with a gentle voice. "The machine is only days old and if you had not bought it out of your own money, then everything that happened yesterday would never have happened at all. Those events are worth more than diamonds to everyone here."

Elizabeth hesitated, momentarily distracted by the front door bell ringing and footsteps in the hall, before replying, "OK then, Abigail, if you're really sure."

"Absolutely, Elizabeth," said Abigail Stratton. Elizabeth folded the cheque and put it in her pocket.

Leaving the office, instead of going back to the kitchen, Miss Stratton headed towards the stairs.

"I thought we were going to the park," Elizabeth said.

"Later," replied Abigail. "First, I would like you to come with me for a moment." Puzzled, Elizabeth followed Abigail Stratton up the stairs. They kept climbing until they reached the door on the third floor.

"Do you trust me?" asked Abigail, standing outside the door.

"Of course," replied Elizabeth, the puzzled expression on her face deepening.

"Then take my hand and close your eyes."

Hesitating for a second, Elizabeth did as she was asked. She heard the door open, felt the movement of air on her face and the pull on her hand. Cautiously she stepped forward, following the gentle tug. She had moved forward by four paces when other unseen hands rested on her shoulders, and with minimal pressure, turned her through ninety degrees. The soft whisper in her ear told her that she could now open her eyes. Blinking, she quickly adjusted her eyes to the light in the room, her hand still held in a warm grip. She gasped, her free hand shot over her mouth, her eyes bulged; she gripped the hand of Abigail Stratton tighter and she stared in total amazement.

There before her, with polished woodwork gleaming, was Peggy.

At first, unable to move, her knees weak, she stretched out her free arm with her fingers straight in longing. She stumbled forward, helped by Abigail until she stood in front of her treasured piano. Oblivious to everything around her, she put her fingertips on the cover and began to caress the surface she had missed so much. She felt the edge of a stool touch the back of her legs and a gentle downward pressure on her shoulders, wanting her to sit. She sank onto the piano stool, her hands immobile on the glistening cover. Curling her fingers, she lifted the lid, exposing those beautiful, familiar ivory-coloured keys. Instinctively, she splayed her fingers over them and gently pressed down. The chord made by Peggy's precious strings took her breath away. She moved her fingers and played another chord. Closing her eyes, her mind, brain, arms and fingers in total harmony, she began to play the moving sonata she loved so much. The sound floated around the room.

She played the final chord. There was a momentary silence before she was snapped out of her dream by the loud clapping she heard behind her. Turning, she saw the children rushing towards her and they threw their arms around with abandon. She saw Abigail Stratton standing by the piano with two gentlemen she didn't know. She recognised the slim, silver-haired person but not the other man next to him. At the same time Brandon and Max left the room.

"Elizabeth," said Abigail Stratton. "That was so, so beautiful. I hope to hear you play your piano many, many times in the future." She noticed the confused look on Elizabeth's face. "Yes dear," she said. "It is your piano. With the great help and inspiration from Mr Riley here," she said gesturing to the Hawk, "this is our gift to you."

Elizabeth could not speak and tears of gratitude trickled down her face. All she could manage was a mouthed, "thank, thank you, oh, thank you." She stood up and wiped the tears from her cheeks with the back of her hand. Abigail introduced Mr Riley to her again and also the man next to him, Mr David Robson. She explained that both of them had been involved since the beginning and told Elizabeth what their functions had been. Elizabeth shook their outstretched hands.

"It is a very great pleasure to meet you at last," said the Hawk. "I had wanted to do so yesterday, but the opportunity did not present itself." Mr Robson echoed the same sentiment.

"We at the Juvenile Support Department have been seriously educated by what you have achieved here," said Mr Robson. "So much so," he continued, "that we have been reviewing our policies and come to the conclusion that what you have done here can be of benefit to other children in our care. We hope that you will agree to become part of this new project." He saw the look of bewilderment on Elizabeth's face. "If you would like to follow me," he said, "I can hopefully explain." He left the room and Elizabeth, arm in arm with Abigail Stratton, followed. The children and everyone else in the room made up the rear guard. Reaching the bottom of the stairs, she did not notice Brandon and Max coming out of the TV room and joining them.

Without a thought about where she was being led, she found herself at the bottom of the outside steps. Looking around slightly confused, as Mr Robson had stopped walking, her eyes fell upon the name board. She gradually realised that there was something different about it. She didn't know that Brandon and Max had left the room to remove a thin, painted plywood cover that the Hawk had arranged to be fitted.

The dawn broke, and the radiance of its pure light with streaming rays, flashed to every corner of her understanding. Her heart missed a beat and a surge of feeling she had never known, enveloped her.

She was home. This is where she belonged. Here was her future and here was her family.

She read the words again.

Saint Etheldreda's
Foundation
&
Music School
Established 1923

About the Author

Martin Varny was born into a music loving family. A very early memory is seeing an old radiogram going up in smoke while playing a 78 rpm record of *Nymph's and Shepherds* sung by the Manchester Children's Choir.

As a boy he sang in a local church choir and also tried to learn to play the piano. Due to short, stiff fingers, he found this difficult, so, after Grade 2, he stopped the piano lessons, much to the relief of his teacher.

School revealed that he had no particular academic talents but he managed to obtain seven "O" levels and left school when he was sixteen.

Now retired, he spent most of his working life in operational functions in marine related industries.

This is his first novel, and the idea for it came "out of the blue" during a conversation about films. The story stayed in his head so he decided to write it down. Typing with one finger in the evenings and weekends, the first original draft was completed in two and a half weeks.

Please Leave a Review

Reviews are so important to writers. Please take the time to review this book. A couple of lines is fine.

Reviews help the book to become more visible to buyers. Retailers will promote books with multiple reviews.

This in turn helps us to sell more books… And then we can afford to publish more books like this one.

Leaving a review is very easy.

Go to https://amzn.to/4bmI7DX, scroll down the left-hand side of the Amazon page and click on the "Write a customer review" button.

Other Publications by The Red Telephone

Navaselva, The Call of the Wild Valley

by Georgina Wright
illustrated by Ruth Koenigsberger

The incredible diversity of our natural world is at risk.

Navaselva calls us to look at our world from the point of view of different wild animal characters. We become aware of their deeper ways of communicating and their challenges on a long journey to the cooler north.

This ecological adventure, framed by our human narrator Jay Ro, brings to life the diverse beauty of nature and shows us the difficulties and fears she faces growing up in the 21st century.

The Call of the Wild Valley, Georgina Wright's first book in the Navaselva series, is a thought-provoking read for the young adult who is curious about our environment.

"Beautifully written, emotive and thought-provoking. A loving and sensitive work of art." *(Amazon)*

Order from Amazon:

Paperback: ISBN 978-1-914199-52-3
eBook: ISBN 978-1-914199-53-0

Where Wild Birds Shriek

by Christian Lea

Harry Burden is classically handsome, wildly eccentric and fiercely intelligent – but he is also the single biggest nitwit Charlie Bloom has ever met. And living together in moneyed London has caused Charlie to grow quite neurotic.

So when Charlie is invited away for the weekend, he considers his options: Sit around insufflating hairspray with Harry, or get away for three days of peace and relaxation. Well, it's no choice at all really. But when Charlie arrives in The Lake District, he quickly discovers that peace and relaxation are not what's in store for him.

Where Wild Birds Shriek is equal parts comedy, drama and madcap farce, featuring sword fights, car crashes, blackbirds, antique duelling pistols, several near-death experiences and a Triumph Bonneville motorcycle.

"Christian Lea is one to watch . The book was great and I was hooked after a day. Looking forward to more from this guy." *(Amazon)*

Order from Amazon:

Paperback: ISBN 978-1-914199-22-6
eBook: ISBN 978-1-914199-23-3

Babel

by Gill James

Babel is the second part of the *Peace Child* series.

Kaleem has found his father and soon finds the love of his life, Rozia Laurence, but he is still not comfortable with his role as Peace Child. He also has to face some of the less palatable truths about his home planet: it is blighted by the existence of the Z Zone, a place where poorer people live outside of society, and by switch-off, compulsory euthanasia for a healthy but aging population, including his mentor, Razjosh.

The Babel Tower still haunts him, but it begins to make sense as he uncovers more of the truth about his past and how it is connected with the problems in the Z Zone.

Kaleem knows he can and must make a difference, but at what personal cost?

Order from Amazon:

Paperback: ISBN 978-1-907335-10-5
eBook: ISBN 978-1-907335-13-6